The Discovery

K.A. Applegate

Hippo

For Grassy Creek Elementary School
And for Michael and Jake

Scholastic Children's Books,
Commonwealth House, 1–19 New Oxford Street, London WC1A 1NU, UK
a division of Scholastic Ltd
London ~ New York ~ Toronto ~ Sydney ~ Auckland
Mexico City ~ New Delhi ~ Hong Kong

First published in the USA by Scholastic Inc., 1998
First published in the UK by Scholastic Ltd, 1999

Copyright © Katherine Applegate, 1998
ANIMORPHS is a trademark of Scholastic Inc.

ISBN 0 439 01179 5

Printed by Cox & Wyman Ltd, Reading, Berks.

10 9 8 7 6 5 4 3 2 1

The Discovery

Sometimes, being a bird can be a problem. . .

BLAM! The window fell shut with a horrendous slam.

BONK! I hit the wall, too distracted to flare. . .

I scooted sideways, centimetre by centimetre.

"Mrrrrrrr-ooowwwrr!"

Uh-oh.

I felt something batting at my exposed talons. I knew what it was.

"Hhhhsssssssss!" the kitty said.

The very big kitty. The big, grey tabby, with its mouth drawn back from needle teeth. . .

> **Even the book morphs!
> Flip the pages
> and check it out!**

Look for other ANIMORPHS titles
by K.A. Applegate:

Chapter 1

My name is Marco.

Her name is T'Shondra.

Isn't that a beautiful name? A beautiful name for a beautiful girl. Which is what I told her as I sidled up casually to her locker.

"T'Shondra," I said.

"Marco," she said.

"A beautiful name for a beautiful girl," I said.

"What is? *Marco?*"

"No, T'Shondra."

"What?"

"T'Shondra. I was just saying I thought it would be a beautiful name for a beautiful girl."

"Oh, really!" she said, giving me serious fish-eye. "It would be, huh? For a *beautiful* girl.

1

But not for me, huh? Is that what you're saying? You just came all the way over here, acting all cool, to tell me I should give my name to some beautiful girl because I'm too much of a *pig* to have the name?"

At this point I could have explained. But I had this bad feeling that the moment was past. You know? Like nothing I could possibly say was going to make this work.

"How about if we just say this conversation never happened?" I suggested. "How about if I just turn and walk away?"

"That would be a good idea."

Now, where was I? Oh yeah, my name is Marco. And I can't tell you my last name or where I live. Why not? Because I'm hoping to live long enough to figure out females, that's why. I mean, is it just me, or are they way too sensitive?

The other day I'm talking to this girl named Danielle. And she happens to work out a lot, so she is very strong. But in a good way. In a *good* way, I emphasize. So I say to her, "Whoa, Danielle, you're looking way buff. Look at those shoulders of yours. You could practically be a boy."

What does she do? Does she say, "Thanks, Marco, for paying me a compliment"? No. She calls over this guy she likes, this guy named Justin Mullins, and says, "Marco just said I look like a boy!"

Well. The end result was me running down the hall yelling, "I meant it in a nice way! Stop chasing me. It was a compliment!"

But that's beside the point. I've been chased by worse than Justin Mullins. I've been chased by Hork-Bajir warriors. I've been chased by Taxxons. I've been chased by Visser Three himself.

Here's the thing you need to understand: life isn't what you think it is. There are things going on that you don't understand.

Earth is being invaded. By some not-nice creatures called Yeerks. They are a parasitic species, like tapeworms. Only they get into your head, not your stomach.

They control you. Utterly. Totally. You're the Muppet and they're the hand. We call people like that Controllers. That's what you are when you're nothing but a human puppet under the control of the Yeerk in your head.

They are everywhere. They can be anyone. You'll never know for sure. Your dad, your mum, your brothers and sisters, the guy who comes to the house and fixes the heating, the smarmy anchorman on the news, the politician, the teacher, the cute little kid. . . There is no way to know. No way to be sure who is, and who is not.

And who is resisting this alien invasion? Who is protecting Earth from this slow-motion, secret conquest by brain-controlling parasites?

Well, prepare to be depressed. Because the

3

only ones fighting the Yeerks are me, four of my friends, and a half-horse, half-scorpion, half-humanoid Andalite we call Ax.

Yes, I know that's too many halves.

The point is, it's me and a handful of my friends trying to save humanity.

Now you're worried, right?

Fortunately, we do have certain powers. We have the ability to become any animal whose DNA we can acquire.

Seriously.

It wasn't something we were born with. We're not freaks. We're not some circus act. We're not the X-Men. Our morphing powers come from Andalite technology. Long story made short: a doomed Andalite prince named Elfangor used a small, blue box to transform us in such a way that we can absorb DNA through touch, and then, just by focusing our thoughts, become that animal.

Obviously, this is technology that is just slightly ahead of human technology. The Andalites are very, very advanced. I hear they even have a Web browser that actually works. Not to mention that whole faster-than-light space-travel thing.

The sad thing is, the thing even I can't joke about, is what happened right after Elfangor gave us this power. That's when Visser Three, the leader of the Yeerk forces on Earth, arrived with Hork-Bajir and human-Controllers and murdered Elfangor.

Visser Three morphed. . . Yes, that's right, he has the morphing power, too. There are millions of Hork-Bajir that have been made into Controllers. And millions of Taxxons. And at least thousands of humans.

But there is only one Andalite-Controller. Just one Yeerk who has an Andalite host body. Just one who has the Andalite morphing power.

Visser Three.

It was Visser Three who morphed into some hideous beast whose DNA he'd acquired on some far-distant world. And, literally, ate Elfangor.

Then they annihilated all traces of Elfangor's ship.

All traces.

Or so I'd thought.

I was walking away from T'Shondra, shaking my head and muttering to myself about females, when I saw it.

I didn't even see the kid holding it at first. I just saw the box.

The blue box.

The morphing cube.

Chapter 2

"Yo!" I said to the boy with the blue box.

I don't know why I said "Yo!" I am not a "Yo!" kind of person. It was all I could think to say. I was too busy having a heart attack to think of anything else.

See, that blue box was supposed to have been destroyed.

That blue box represented more power than half the weapons in the world combined. That little blue box could give anyone morphing power.

The Yeerks would do anything to get it. And when I say "anything" I mean some things you don't even want to think about.

So I said "Yo!"

And the kid stopped walking. He looked at

me like maybe he should know me but couldn't quite remember me.

He was a little taller than me. Most people are. He had blond hair and brown eyes and a look on his face like maybe he had an attitude.

"What?" he asked me.

"Um . . . I don't know you, do I?" I said.

"I'm new," he said.

"Ah," I remarked. Normally words come easily to me. But I was in brain-lock. I kept scanning round the crowded hallway, looking for Jake. Or Cassie. Someone with some sense. Not Rachel. Rachel's idea of dealing with this kid would probably involve dragging him into the nearest cupboard, morphing into her grizzly bear morph, and getting that blue box the quick and direct way.

But I didn't see Jake. Or Cassie. Or even Rachel.

"So. My name is Marco."

"I'm David."

"David! OK. Good name."

David gave me a look like maybe I was an idiot. And to be honest with you, I wasn't doing much to change his opinion.

"Later," he said and started to walk away.

"Hey, David!" I yelled after him. "What's that blue thing?"

He turned back towards me. "I don't know. I found it. It was in that construction site over

7

across from the shopping mall. In a hole in a wall. Inside the cement block. Like it had been put in there or something."

"Yeah?"

"Yeah. It's weird. I mean, it feels like it must be something, you know? Like it's not just a plain old box. It has some writing on it. Like it might be foreign, or something."

BRRRRRIIIIINNNNNGGGGGG!

The gentle sound of the bell made me leap approximately half a metre in the air.

"Hey! Can I have it? I mean, it looks cool and all. I could pay you. . ." I began turning my pockets out. Fluff balls . . . a very old peppermint Life Saver. . .

"I could pay you a dollar and thirty-two cents," I offered lamely, holding out the bill, the coins, and the Life Saver.

"Marco, huh?" the kid said.

"Yeah. I'm Marco. Nice to meet you."

"Even nicer to say goodbye," he said.

He walked away. And then, too late, I spotted Jake. I went right up to him, grabbed him by the jacket, and yanked him into the boys' toilet.

"Some kid has the blue box!" I hissed.

"What blue box?" he demanded, shoving me back.

"*The* blue box." I crouched to look under the stall doors and make sure we were alone. "Elfangor's blue box."

8

Jake's face went pale. "Oh—"
BRRRRRIIIIINNNNNGGGGGG!

Chapter 3

We were in the barn. Cassie's barn. Also known as the Wildlife Rehabilitation Clinic. Cassie's parents are both vets. And she's very into animals, too.

In fact, while the rest of us were busy panicking, she was calmly shoving pills down the throat of an enormous swan.

"How did that blue box manage to survive?" Rachel demanded. "The Yeerks Draconed Elfangor's fighter until it was dust. We were there. We watched it happen."

We all turned to look at Ax. Sometimes Ax doesn't attend meetings. But we needed him here for this one. He was in his own, fabulously strange Andalite body: blue and brown fur, weak arms, too many fingers, four hooves, nasty bullwhip tail, no mouth, and two extra eyeballs mounted on stalks that look this way and that.

Ax is our expert on all alien weirdness. What with being a weird alien himself.

"What do you think happened, Ax?" Jake asked him.

<I do not know,> Ax said, using Andalite thought-speak.

"What do you mean, you don't know?" Rachel said. "Is there something special about those blue boxes, like they can't be destroyed by Dracon beams?"

<No. It could be destroyed by a Dracon beam. All I can suggest is that maybe it was a simple incident of random chance.>

"Is that Andalite-ese for a freak accident?" I asked.

<Yes. The Dracon beam striking my brother's fighter would have created explosive pressures. Perhaps this pressure simply hurled the Escafil Device away at high speed.>

<The what?> Tobias asked.

Tobias was in his usual place: up in the rafters where he can see out through the hayloft. Tobias is one of us, but not exactly one of us. He's what the Andalites call a *nothlit*. That's a person who's been trapped in a morph because they stayed in it for more than two hours.

Long story.

Anyway, Tobias is a red-tailed hawk. And

11

during these little get-togethers he uses his laser-focus hawk eyes and excellent hawk hearing to make sure no one sneaks up on us without our knowing it.

<It is called an Escafil Device. Actually, it has a number of names. Escafil was the inventor of morphing technology. You know, the science behind it is quite incredible. The device causes a cascading cellular regeneration tied to a Z-space —>

"We so do *not* care!" I said. "It can cascade all over its Z-space for all I care. The point is, this thing, this box, this device, this morphing cube, currently belongs to some kid named David who thinks I'm an idiot!"

Rachel nodded thoughtfully. "Well, if he thinks Marco's an idiot he can't be all bad." She batted her eyelashes at me to show she was kidding.

I love it when she does that.

"We need to get this box," I said.

"Yep," Jake agreed. "We do."

"Before he figures out what it is," Cassie said, speaking up for the first time. "And more important, before the Yeerks discover he has it."

I took a good, long look at Cassie. See, there was this little episode with Cassie. She quit the Animorphs because I guess she had problems with some of the stuff we have to do.

She came back, of course. But since then I'd

felt a little shaky around her. Cassie has way too many morals and ethics. She's always wondering whether something is right or wrong. Me, I just wonder "will it work?" or not.

I was thinking of something snide to say to Cassie, but I decided to keep my mouth shut. Cassie has saved my life more than once. You cut a person a lot of slack when they've saved your life.

"OK, so we need information," Jake said. "We need to know where this kid lives, most of all. Then we go in and get the blue box."

<And we have to be careful not to let the kid even suspect what's going on,> Tobias said.

"And obviously we have to be careful not to hurt David," Jake said. "He's an innocent by-stander."

"No problem-o," Rachel said. "He's not a Hork-Bajir, he's not a Taxxon, and he's not Visser Three. Us versus some kid from school? Puh-leeze. It's a walk in the park."

Normally, I have a superstition about ever saying something is going to be easy. But this time, even I didn't worry.

Now I have a new superstition: any time I'm not worried, I worry.

Chapter 4

We waited in the outdoor seating area of a Burger King down the street. Just four of us. Ax would have been slightly obvious, and there was no way to trust him in human morph anywhere near grease and salt. Tobias was off scouting out David's house.

It was night, but there was plenty of light: cars driving by, a weird glow from the used car lot across the street, and the big Burger King sign itself.

It was chilly, so we were dressed warmly. Kind of a problem, since, if we were going to morph, we'd lose our clothes. So we'd worked out a plan. Two of us would stay behind, one boy, one girl. We'd shed the outer clothes in the rest rooms, then the two who were staying back would hold on to them.

It is so annoying not being able to morph outer clothing.

"Short chip stays here," I said. I broke two chips in half. I put one short and one long in my fist. "All right, Jake. Grab a chip."

He pulled out a short one.

"Looks like I'm going and you are pulling toilet duty," I said cheerfully.

Cassie and Rachel drew, too. Rachel won. Or lost, depending on your point of view.

"You and me, Xena," I said.

Rachel arched one eyebrow at me. "You know, if I'm Xena, what's that make you?"

"Hercules, obviously."

"I was thinking more Joxer. Isn't that the annoying weenie who hangs around Xena?"

"OK, that does it." I stuck my elbow up on the table, arm upright in the arm-wrestling position. "Let's go. Come on, let's settle this once and for all."

Jake yawned. "Shouldn't we have a pair of live scorpions to make it interesting?"

Rachel grinned and stuck her arm up alongside mine. Our hands clasped. I pushed. She pushed. And then. . .

"Ow!" A sudden, sharp pain in my knee.

An instant later my hand slammed down on the table.

"You kicked me! She kicked me under the

15

table! Jake, your cousin kicked me!"

Rachel laughed. "Who cares how you win as long as you win?"

Cassie rolled her eyes. "You don't really believe that, Rachel. No, wait a minute, you probably do."

"Good grief, the two of you off alone on this mission?" Jake muttered. "Instead of *Dumb and Dumber* it's *Crazy and Crazier*."

Rachel and I looked at each other and both burst out laughing.

"*Crazy and Crazier*," Rachel repeated, deliberately laughing crazily.

"Yeah, but which of us is which?"

I looked up and saw a kid walking towards us. He was carrying a burger bag.

I got serious in a hurry. "Erek," I said to Jake.

Erek King is this kid who used to go to our school. At least, that's what he looks like, acts like, and sounds like. But every part of Erek you see is a holographic projection. The real Erek is inside the hologram. The real Erek is an android.

Erek is one of the Chee, a very, very old race of androids created by the long-dead Pemalites. The Chee are unable to commit any violent act, despite being frighteningly powerful. But they hate the Yeerks and love humans. Or, actually, they love dogs, and they love humans because we love dogs, too.

Another long story.

Bottom line is that the Chee are allies of ours who are amazingly good at infiltrating the Yeerks.

"Hey, Erek," Jake said calmly.

Rachel nodded. Cassie smiled.

"Hi, guys, what's up?" Erek said, sounding exactly like any normal kid, rather than a robot so old he helped build the pyramids.

"Not much," I said, cutting off Cassie before she could explain what we were up to. We trust the Chee, but there's no point giving out any more information than is necessary.

I'm suspicious by nature.

"What's up with you, Erek?" Jake asked.

Erek took out a Whopper and unwrapped it. He took a big bite and chewed it. I knew that in reality the food would simply be incinerated inside Erek's android body.

"No cheese?" I asked him.

He shook his head and grinned. "I try and keep my fat intake down."

"Yeah. Right. You want to live to the ripe old age of, what, a billion years?"

Erek laughed again. Then he put down the burger. "Something big is happening. No one knows about this yet. It's not going to be announced publicly until it's all over. For security reasons."

"What's happening?" Rachel asked eagerly, leaning forward.

17

"Oh, nothing much," the android said coyly. "Just a summit meeting right here in town. The presidents or prime ministers of Britain, France, Russia, Japan, Germany and the United States are all coming here to figure out what to do about all the problems in the Middle East."

"Uh-huh," Rachel said, unimpressed. "So?"

"It's the ultimate target," Cassie said. "The leaders of six powerful nations? All in one place at one time? Right here, where the Yeerk invasion is strongest?"

Jake leaned closer to Erek. "You have any reason to believe the Yeerks are thinking about going after all these guys?"

Erek nodded. "The planning is under way. The presidents and prime ministers start arriving the day after tomorrow. They'll be staying at the big Marriott resort down the coast."

"This could be an opportunity," Cassie said thoughtfully. "If we could reach these leaders somehow, show them, prove to them what's happening. . . I mean, the Yeerks could be totally exposed."

"And on the flip side, if the Yeerks make Controllers of these guys, that's the ball game, we're done," I pointed out.

"One big problem," Erek said.

"Just one?" I said.

"OK, lots of big problems, and one huge problem," Erek said, not smiling his holographic smile. "One of the leaders is already a Controller. Make the wrong move, approach the wrong leader, and. . ."

He let it hang.

"You don't know which leader is the Controller?" Jake asked.

Erek shook his head. "If we did, it'd just be a big problem, not a huge one."

Chapter 5

Erek left and the four of us just sat there staring at each other. None of us wanted to think about a world where the presidents of the United States and most of the other major powers were slaves of the Yeerks.

We'd have to try and stop them.

"OK, one thing at a time," Jake said. "We deal with this blue box situation first."

Suddenly, I felt something pass by overhead. Tobias swooped over and landed on the "R" in Burger King.

<No problem,> he reported. <Kid's window is wide open. I can see the blue box sitting on his desk. In and out. I'd have just done it myself, but you said to report back.>

Jake nodded like he was nodding to me.

Thought-speak only works when you're in morph. Tobias could do it. We couldn't.

Tobias cocked his head and stared harder. <OK, who died? You all look like you just got news that the school holiday's been cancelled. Never mind, tell me later.>

In a conversational tone of voice Jake said, "OK, well, let's get this over with. Rachel and Marco? Let's go."

We went inside, looking like any normal group of kids. Me and Jake went to the men's room. It was a small, single-stall room. There was no one else in there. We locked the door.

I shucked off my sweatshirt. "Don't lose that shirt," I said. "It was signed by Steve Young."

"Marco, it was signed like two years ago and you've washed it at least once since then. The name is totally invisible now."

"I didn't say it was still signed, did I? I said it *was* signed. It has sentimental value."

Jake looked around at the gloomy surroundings. "Just part of the glamour of life as a superhero."

"Yeah, what happened to those big, walk-in phone boxes the old Superman always changed in?"

"You know, I still just can't get used to the new Superman," Jake said.

I began to focus on the morph. This was an airmail job. Bird-time. In through the window, snatch up the box, and zoom right back out.

No problem-o, as Rachel had said. Nothing to worry about, especially when compared to what Erek had just told us.

I was very familiar with the morph, an osprey. Ospreys are a kind of hawk. Normally they live near water and eat fish. Very rarely do they hang out in men's toilets at Burger King.

I focused my mind and began to shrink. The urinal was suddenly eye level and Jake was looking even larger than usual.

Bomp! Bomp! Bomp! At the door.

"There's someone in here!" Jake yelled.

I continued morphing. My skin turned grey. Grey like a dirty blackboard. Like I'd been dead for a couple of weeks. It's very disturbing to look down and see your skin turn grey, let me tell you.

But not as disturbing as when the feather patterns appear like line drawings and then sort of flake up, going 3-D.

My fingers stretched out, elongating compared to the rest of my hands and arms. As they elongated, though, they slipped right out of the skin so that they became dry, white, bird-bone.

"Eeeewww!" Jake said, laughing in disgust. "That's something new!"

"Oh, man, I don't need to ever see that again!" I said.

Morphing is very unpredictable. It's not just

this sort of gradual thing. It goes through phases. Sudden, bizarre, totally gross-looking stages.

The bare bones thing was something new. And deeply, deeply not pretty.

Bomp! Bomp! Bomp! Bomp! Bomp!

"Is someone in there?" a voice demanded.

"Yeah, someone is in here!" Jake yelled. "Jeez!"

"Come outta there, right now!"

"What?" Jake demanded.

"Whackl?" I demanded, having just that moment had my lips turn into hard beak.

"Are you kids in there doing drugs?" the voice demanded.

"No!" Jake looked down at me, exasperated. "Hurry up."

"GET OUT HERE, NOW!"

A new voice. A very authoritative voice. I heard the sound of a key turning in the lock.

"Stop morphing!" Jake hissed. "Stand up straight and keep quiet!"

I stood there, about ninety per cent osprey. I was just under a metre tall, standing on my talons.

Jake swept the sweatshirt over me. He pulled the hood over my head and yanked the string.

The door opened. Two people stood there, glaring at us. A teenager in a Burger King uniform. And a manager.

"I'm just trying to let my little brother go to

the toilet," Jake said, patting me on the shoulder.

The kid and the man both looked down at me. I was standing inside a sweatshirt that was so huge it lay in folds around my feet. Which was a good thing, since my feet were talons. The arms hung limp.

"Your little brother?" the manager asked. "Why's his sweatshirt so big?"

"Hey, that sweatshirt was signed by Steve Young!" Jake said. Like that was an explanation.

"Something's wrong with his face!" the kid said.

Jake put his arm around me protectively. "Don't listen to them, Tommy," he said, with a sob in his voice. "Your face is just fine! It's just fine, I tell you! The doctors say some day you may be normal again."

"Hey, I didn't mean anything by. . ." the kid said.

"What is it?" the manager asked in a concerned tone. "I mean, his disease."

Jake went blank. "Um. . ."

<Beakanoma,> I whispered to Jake in thought-speak.

"Beakanoma," Jake said.

<A growth in the shape of a beak,> I explained.

"It's a, uh, a growth in the shape of a beak," Jake said.

<It's especially tragic and all because it only afflicts really smart, really cute people,> I said.

"Oh, shut up," Jake muttered under his breath.

Jake hustled me away. As fast as I could walk on talons while wearing a massive sweatshirt.

Chapter 6

David lived in a basic kind of home: two storeys, a lawn, a garden with a barbecue and a rusty swing set. Also a pool.

I was instantly jealous. I don't have a pool.

He had one of the upstairs bedrooms.

Tobias, Rachel and I zoomed past the house at an altitude of twenty metres or so. I could see why Tobias doesn't like to fly at night. In the darkness hawk eyes aren't much better than human eyes. And after the sun goes down you start losing the thermals, the warm updraughts that make flying easier.

So it was hard flapping to cover the few blocks from Burger King to David's house. And talk about confusing. You ever tried to tell one house from the next at night? From twenty metres in the air? Not easy. But the pool was lit, and in fact, David was in the water, swimming back and forth.

His room was brightly lit, which helped us see, and I easily spotted the blue cube on his desk.

<OK, I'm going in!> Rachel said.

<Uh-uh, I don't think so,> Tobias said. <You're too big in that bulky eagle morph. You can't fly through that window. Me and Marco had better go.>

<Oh, man!> Rachel complained. But even she could see Tobias was right.

<Give us a warning if David gets out of the pool,> Tobias said. Then he spilled air from his wings and stabilized on a glide path, straight for the bright rectangle of the window.

But I managed to get out ahead of him. <Hah!> I said.

<Marco! Careful if you're going first. You'll need to flare as soon as you pass the window-sill. I mean instantly, or you'll smack the far wall.>

<Hey, I'm not as experienced as you are, Tobias, but I'm not a complete idiot.>

<No, you're an *in*complete idiot!> Rachel called down helpfully.

I zoomed, down, down through the night, aimed straight for that window. It was cool. Like what it must be like to land a jet on an aircraft carrier at night. Just a little, glowing target in the darkness.

<Make sure you stay clear of that stick,> Tobias said. He was just two metres behind me.

<What stick?> I asked, and then the window was suddenly right in front of me! It was a trick of the light! It had seemed further away.

I tried to slow down, ready to flare once I was in. And then I saw the stick. The stick that was propping the window open.

Thwack! My left wing hit the stick.

<Wha!> I yelled.

BLAM! The window fell shut with a horrendous slam.

Bonk! Tobias hit the closed window.

BONK! I hit the wall, too distracted to flare.

I hit, I fell, I landed behind a dresser. I was wedged in a space of about seven centimetres, unable to move. All I could do was slowly slither down to the carpet.

<Tobias!> Rachel cried.

<I'm OK,> Tobias said. <Professor Plum did it in the conservatory with the candlestick!>

Tobias was alive. But he must have hit fairly hard. He seemed to be reliving a game of Cluedo.

I wasn't exactly in great shape myself. I scooted sideways, centimetre by centimetre.

"Mrrrrrrr-ooowwwrr!"

Uh-oh.

I scooted faster. Faster, desperate to get out from behind the dresser.

I felt something batting at my exposed talons. I knew what it was.

One wing free! Then my body. And then. . .

"Hhhhsssssssss!" the kitty said.

The very big kitty. The big, grey tabby, with its mouth drawn back from needle teeth.

<Good kitty,> I said. <Gooood kitty.>

The kitty didn't like big birds in its bedroom. And it really didn't like big talking birds in its bedroom.

"MmmmrrrrOOOOWWWWWRRR!" Kitty said, explaining its feelings to me.

<Miss Scarlet? Was it Miss Scarlet with the plum in the professor?> Tobias wondered.

<Marco! Get out of there!> Rachel yelled. <I saw a cat.>

<Yeah. I kind of noticed him,> I said.

We've all seen house cats. I've seen lots of house cats. But they look radically different when you're a bird. Even a big, tough, predatory bird.

Slash!

The cat swiped at my wing, claws extended.

<OK, Mr Kitty, you want to do this? You want to throw down? Fine. I'll kick your butt!>

Mr Kitty was not impressed. Mr Kitty jumped. He went from being twenty centimetres away to being zero centimetres away in just about a billionth of a second.

<Aaaaahhhh!> I yelled.

"MrrrOOOOWWW-hsssssss!" the cat said.

Suddenly it was a wild tangle of claws and talons and beaks and teeth and I swear we must have looked like one of those cartoons where Bugs Bunny and Yosemite Sam are fighting and all you see is swirling dust and cartoon stars.

We fell apart, glaring and panting at each other. I had got in a few good hits. But Mr Kitty was fast. And Mr Kitty had clawed my belly down to the skin, bitten me in the neck, wing, other wing, and left leg. All in approximately six seconds.

I wasn't up for a second round. I did not want my obituary to say "died from injuries sustained while battling a fat house cat". That would be embarrassing.

I could demorph. Or I could escape.

Out through the shut window? No.

Through the closed door? No.

Which left demorphing.

Except that right then Rachel decided to rescue me.

CRASH!

The window exploded! In blew a rock, followed by a massive bald eagle, wings folded.

She flared. Her wings practically stretched from wall to wall. She landed on the bed.

"Rooowwwrr!" Mr Kitty said in a very surprised voice.

<Come on, let's bail!> Rachel yelled.

And that's when the door slammed open. In came David. The cat screeched and leaped on to the curtains beside the window.

<Out the door!> Rachel said.

<I'm with you!> I said. <We have to grab that cube!>

<I'll distract David. You grab it!> Rachel said. She began flapping her wings madly and lashing all around with her talons.

"Whoa!" David yelled.

Rachel began tearing up the pillows. Feathers fluttered round the room. The cat was climbing towards the ceiling. I hopped and flapped over to the desk. The cube! There it was!

David lurched to the desk, like he was going to attack me. But instead he yanked open a drawer and whipped out. . .

<A gun! A gun? This kid has a gun?!> I yelped.

From far off I heard, <Actually, Miss Scarlet, I think you should have used the wrench.>

Chapter 7

<Gun? What gun?> Rachel yelled.

Pop! Pop! Pop!

Something stung my bare belly. <He's got a pellet gun!>

<He could put someone's eye out with that!> Rachel cried in outrage.

<Yeah, mine!> I said. I closed one talon over the cube. It was too big! I used both talons. I could hold the cube, but I could barely stand. I flapped like a madman and managed to fall off the desk, still holding the cube.

Pop! Pop!

<OK, now he's ticked me off!> Rachel said.

<Don't hurt him!> I said. <He's just an innocent bystander.>

<Innocent, my—>

Pop! Pop! Pop!

I flapped hard and scooted along the carpet towards the door. Rachel did a little better, but once in the hallway her wings hit the walls with each stroke.

"Oh no, you don't!" David yelled. "Give me back that blue box!"

Off we went: two dragging, scuffling, staggering, pellet-stung birds, one hauling a blue box. Followed by an outraged boy yelling and firing a very life-like gun.

Down the hall!

<Ow!>

<Look out!>

"Give me back my box!"

Pop! Pop! Pop!

Down the stairs!

<Ow!>

<Hey, watch it!>

"Give me back my box!"

Pop! Pop! Pop!

Through the empty family room where the TV was on, showing *Buffy the Vampire Slayer*.

<Whoa, I forgot to set the VCR!> I said. <We're missing *Buffy*.>

Pop! Pop! Pop!

<Owww! Oh man, I am so going to find a way to hurt this kid tomorrow at school,> Rachel threatened. <I'm going for the sliding glass door. Distract him while I get it open.>

<Distract him? By doing what? You figure I should do my Lord of the Dance impersonation?>

Rachel grabbed the sliding glass door handle with her beak and yanked. David ran straight for me. Straight for the box.

I could either jump up and rake his eyeballs, or give up the box. But David was not a Controller. He was not an enemy. And even I don't think you can just go around tearing into innocent bystanders.

I jumped back from the box. The door slid open. And Rachel and I flapped across the back lawn, over the pool, above the fence, and out of there.

"Yeah! And don't come back, either!" David yelled as he fired off a final pellet.

<I am so not looking forward to explaining this to Jake,> Rachel said.

<We got our butts kicked by a kid with a pellet gun. That's just pathetic.>

A hawk rose up to join us.

<Tobias?>

<Yeah. Man, that was a bad bump I took. I was having this weird dream. I was trapped in the conservatory with Professor Plum. So, how'd everything go?>

Chapter 8

It was not our finest hour. We backed off, regrouped, and decided to try again the next evening after David had calmed down. We still had to get that blue box back before dealing with the much bigger problem of how to save the leaders of the free world.

Plus, I was supposed to be doing an extra science paper to replace the paper I'd forgotten to do last week.

The next day was another school day. You know the routine: get up way too early, shower, dress, stand around waiting for the bus with the usual collection of dorks, try to cram for the first-period test while the bouncing bus bruises your butt bones.

Then it's that first sight of the school

building, followed, in my case at least, by a sinking sensation. Then you spot some cute girl who hasn't called you "Beavis" yet and you start thinking, *OK, I guess I can stand another day.*

Common room. Class. Class. Lunch.

The long wait in line as the aroma of something dead wafts towards you. Brussels sprouts? Aubergine? No, it's cauliflower.

"You said your name is Marco, right?"

I swivelled around but continued to push my plastic tray along the line. It was David. I jerked like a guilty perpetrator being questioned by Lieutenant Sipowicz.

"Yeah. Marco," I said. "David, right?"

He nodded. Then he looked at the food steaming and reeking. "The food was better at my last school."

"That would pretty much have to be true. It couldn't be any worse. Not unless your last school was a prison."

He didn't laugh. He just looked at me kind of intensely. "I don't have any friends here yet. Something really weird happened to me yesterday. Very weird. Want to hang?"

"Sure. So, what—"

"Cauliflower or green bean casserole?" the lunch lady asked me. "Come on, little Marco, let's keep it moving."

"The casserole definitely," I said. "It sounds so French and all." I turned to David and said,

"You know the English word for casserole? Slop."

Again, no laugh.

We got our food and threaded our way through the boisterous zoo that was the dining room. There were a couple of empty tables at the far side of the room. I sat down. David sat across from me.

I had to act cool, not too interested in his story. It was easy because I basically knew all about it.

"Remember that blue box I showed you yesterday?"

I pretended to think. "Yeah. Now I do, yeah."

He leaned forward. "Last night someone tried to steal it. And you'll never guess how they did it. Trained birds."

"Say what?"

"Two birds flew in my bedroom window and tried to get away with the box. Fortunately my cat, Megadeth, went after one."

"You named your cat Megadeth?"

"I just wish my snake had been out of his box. He's had his venom taken out, but I bet it would have scared those birds."

"Snake?"

"Yeah, he's really cool. He's a cobra. You're not even supposed to be able to own them, but my dad got it for me. He goes overseas a lot. He's a spy. But don't tell anyone."

37

This was getting to be a lot to absorb. A cat named Megadeth, a cobra, and a father who was possibly a spy?

"Ooookay," I said.

"Look, I know it sounds weird and all, but those birds were not ordinary birds. One of them opened a sliding glass door. It was an eagle, I think."

"Why would anyone want to steal that blue box?"

He shook his head. "I don't know. But it must be valuable, right? Or else why would someone go to all the trouble of using trained birds?"

I nodded. "Makes sense." Yeah, right. Makes perfect sense: burglar birds. There are times when I realize my real life has got so insane that I can't even be sure what is truly insane.

"Anyway, I bet it's worth a lot of money, so I'm going to try and sell it."

That sent a nice chill up my spine. "Sell it?"

"Yeah. I posted a 'for sale' notice on a couple of Web pages last night after all this went down. I described it. And I described those symbols, the ones that look like foreign writing? This morning before school I checked, and there was already an answer. Some guy says he wants to see it. He says he'll pay good money. Says he'll go anywhere, any time."

That did more than give me a chill. That stopped my breathing for about ten seconds.

"You did what?"

"I'm thinking I should have some back-up, you know? Someone to cover me, in case anything goes down. You're the only guy I know here."

"You didn't give this guy your address, did you?"

David smirked. "I'm not a moron. The guy could just rip me off while I'm stuck here at school." He shook his head and gave me a sly leer. "I set it up on a timer so the E-mail with my address won't go out until right before I get home."

"It's on automatic?" I said.

He nodded. "I send the E-mail, the guy comes over, and I give you ten per cent for helping me out."

"Good plan," I said as calmly as I could. But inside I was having a very different thought that went something like, *You IDIOT FREAK! Do you know WHO is going to show up looking for that box?*

Of course I didn't say that.

I spotted Jake heading over in my direction. I gave him a small shake of my head, and he turned away.

David rattled on, telling the story of the bird invasion. Then moving on to plans for spending the money he was going to make. But I wasn't listening.

In a couple of hours the E-mail was going to be sent. And very, very soon after that, David was going to get a visitor he didn't want to meet.

I sat there, looking at David and thinking, *How in the world am I going to save your life?*

Chapter 9

I told Jake later during class. He jerked upright, said a word you really shouldn't say in class, and was sent to discuss the matter with the principal.

I spent part of the afternoon finding an opportunity to tell Rachel and Cassie. I had to wait until they were together. Cassie has a calming influence on Rachel.

One thing was clear: we didn't want that E-mail going out. Which meant I was going to be missing the last two periods. Jake made the final decision between fifth and sixth period, by my locker.

"Do it," he said. "Bail. And get to that kid's computer. Kill that E-mail."

"He may have security on it, a password," I

pointed out. "Maybe I'll swing by and try to get Ax to come along."

Jake nodded. "You're not going to have much time. Better haul. You can use my notes from class later."

"Thanks," I said. "But I think I'll use Cassie's notes. Yours will be all covered with doodles and pictures of jets and tanks."

I know how to get up to the roof of the school, and fortunately, no one was up there. I shoved my outer clothing into my backpack. I'd have to get it later. In five minutes I was in the air.

I knew I was on a desperate, life-and-death mission. But that couldn't totally erase the absolute joy I felt on pushing off from the school roof and feeling the air beneath my wings.

I mean, I'm sorry, but haven't you ever sat in school, wishing you could zoom off into the wild blue? It was just so cool. As long as I didn't consider the possibility that the school might call my dad.

That took away a little of the pleasure.

Plus, the possibility that before this day was over I'd be fighting Visser Three.

And yet it was a mostly sunny day, with some huge cumulus clouds piled kilometres high in the sky. And the warm air radiating up off the ground lifted me effortlessly higher and higher. Higher and higher, until the houses looked like shoe boxes and cars looked like Matchbox toys.

I turned towards the distant line of forest. It wouldn't be easy finding Ax. He kept out of sight during the day. We were worried some deer hunter would spot him and try to shoot. Or worse, that some Controller might spot him and know what he was.

Now I began to realize that the breeze was blowing against me. Which meant slow going. But Tobias had taught us that sometimes altitude makes up for ground speed. See, if you get high enough, you can use gravity to let you swoop long distances, even against the wind. It's like climbing to the top of a really tall slide. Even if the wind is against you, you can slide to the bottom.

I rode a thermal up and up, as high as I've ever flown. I don't know how far. But far enough that I spotted a small private plane at my same altitude.

I took aim on the forest and went into a long, gentle glide that eventually brought me to my target.

Ax hangs out in about twenty-five square kilometres of forest. You have any idea how much forest that is? A lot. That's a lot of trees. My osprey eyes saw everything, down to the beetles and worms down on the dead leaves.

But even I couldn't see Ax. Not for a long time. Too long.

Now I was nervous. Now I was definitely nervous. I'd been in morph for over an hour, and even when I found Ax I'd have to fly all the way back to—

A flash of movement below!

A deer. No! Not a deer. Not unless deer were turning blue.

I spilled air and headed down.

<Ax! Ax! Is that you? It's me, Marco.>

He stopped running. I was close enough now to see one stalk eye swivel up towards the sky and focus on me.

<Shouldn't you be in school?> he asked.

<What are you, the truant officer? I need your help. Do you think you could get past whatever security someone might have on a PC?>

Ax laughed. Then he stopped. <Oh, you are serious. I assumed you were making a joke. I am making an effort to recognize human humour and respond appropriately.>

<Uh-huh.> I landed pretty well on a fallen log, digging my talons into rotting wood and exciting a bunch of termites. <So, can you do it?>

<Of course I can do it,> Ax said. <A human computer? I know you don't mean to insult me, but really, even asking the question is an insult to any Andalite.>

I sighed. <What ever. You need to morph. We need to haul butt.>

<What is the problem?> Ax asked. But he wasn't wasting time. He was already melting, shifting, morphing.

<It's the blue box. If I'm right, in about an hour Visser Three is going to get an E-mail offering him a chance to buy it.>

Chapter 10

Tick-tock. Tick-tock. Time was running out fast.

The wind was with us on our trip back to David's house. Just one problem: have you ever tried to find one house in the middle of a whole block of almost identical houses? From the air? When the only other time you've seen the place was at night?

<Are you lost?> Ax asked me.

<No, *we* are lost,> I said. <Look for a pool. It was sort of kidney-shaped.>

<A pool? A Yeerk pool?>

<No, just a human pool.>

<I've never heard of such a thing. Are they necessary for reproduction?>

<No. But they help you get friends during the summer.>

I spotted a blue, kidney-shaped pool and veered towards it. It looked right. Surely it was the right place.

Only just across the street was an identical house with an identical pool.

I could have cried from sheer frustration. Then, from up above us, came a thought-speak voice. <Ax? And who, Marco? Cassie?>

<Tobias!> I yelled. <What are you doing up there? And how did you know it was us?>

<What I'm doing is riding this excellent thermal. And any idiot would know there's something weird about a northern harrier and an osprey zipping around peeking in people's windows. Good grief. Have you ever heard the word "subtle"?>

<Make fun of me later,> I snapped. <We need to find David's house. Like now!>

<A block to the west,> Tobias said. <Hang tight, I'll show you.>

Down he fell, like a missile coming down on its target. Ax and I flapped to intercept him.

<What's the deal?> Tobias asked.

<He's offering the box for sale over the Internet. He already has one interested party. There's a timed E-mail we have to stop. But I'm worried he'll have it protected by a password. That's why I brought Ax.>

<Ah. Um . . . if there's a password, why not just turn off the computer?>

I almost splatted into the rooftop from sheer "duh".

<Oh. I guess we could do that,> I said, feeling like possibly the biggest idiot in the world. Of course, duh: turn off the computer. Or at least yank out the phone cord.

I hate feeling like an idiot.

<It would still be best if we made it look like the E-mail went out. Then if David doesn't get an answer he'll figure, you know, no one was interested.>

<How do we get inside the house?> Tobias asked. <All the windows are closed. I'm not splatting into any more windows.>

We were circling above the house, three birds of prey, probably looking like vultures or something. Tobias was right. The windows were all closed. There was plywood in the window Rachel had busted the day before.

I was feeling a little more relaxed now. We had a little more than an hour before the E-mail would go out. Plenty of time.

<OK, here's what we do. Ax and I will morph to cockroach and crawl in under the back door. Tobias, you stay and make sure nothing eats us.>

Ax and I landed in the back garden. There was a nice, high fence, which was good. And we'd looked in every window and were sure no one was home.

I demorphed by the rusty swing set. In a few minutes Ax and I were ourselves. We walked over to the back door. I knelt down to take a look at the crack beneath the door. There was plenty of room for a cockroach.

"OK, let's get this over with," I said. I rested my hand on the doorknob, preparing to enter cockroach morph. But then I felt the doorknob slip.

"Hey, these people left the door unlocked," I said. "Come on."

<Nooooo!> Tobias yelled, just as I pushed the door open.

"What's the matter?" I said. "It's open, so—"

WwwwAAAAHHHHH! WwwwAAAAHHHHH!

<Burglar alarm, that's what's the matter!> Tobias yelled.

<What is that unpleasantly loud sound?> Ax wondered.

"Oh, man!" I yelled. "Come on! Let's go! Tobias, let us know if you see cops showing up!"

I rushed inside, with Ax trotting along behind me.

Through the kitchen, with Ax's hooves skittering wildly on the vinyl.

WwwwAAAAHHHHH! WwwwAAAAHHHHH!

Through the carpeted living room.

Crash! Ax's tail had caught a lamp. A ceramic lamp. Which was now *pieces* of ceramic lamp.

WwwwAAAAHHHHH! WwwwAAAAHHHHH!

Up the stairs.

Crash! Crash! Crash! Three little, framed pictures mounted on the stairway walls were swept clean by Ax's tail.

WwwwAAAAHHHHH! WwwwAAAAHHHHH!

"This is working out great!" I yelled in frustration.

<Marco! Ax! Someone's pulling up!>

Into David's room. The computer monitor showed a cool screen saver. I bumped the mouse. Off went the screen saver. I double-clicked on the AOL icon.

Deedly-deedly-deeedly! The phone rang and I jumped about a metre straight up.

WwwwAAAAHHHHH! WwwwAAAAHHHHH!

Deedly-deed—

Someone had answered the phone! I shot a look at Ax. It wasn't him.

WwwwAAAAHHHHH! Wwww—

Someone had turned off the alarm!

And from downstairs I heard a strong, male voice say, "Yes, I'm home now and the alarm was going off. (Pause.) I'm sure I can handle it. (Pause.) No, I'm a law enforcement officer. No need to send one of your guards out here. I'll check it out."

Click.

David's father, obviously. Home from work. Home from work as a "law enforcement officer". Home from work with his gun.

50

I glanced at the screen. The AOL software was loading up. Slowly.

No time to wait. We had to hide. We had to hide me, plus a big, blue scorpion-looking, deer-boy from outer space. And we had to hide us from a guy who knew how to search.

Great.

"Ax! Into the cupboard and morph something small!" I hissed.

He leaped. I leaped, too, straight underneath the desk. I was going to yank the phone wire out, just to be safe.

But David's desk was one of those desks that has a back piece. I couldn't get to the wires.

"OK, if anyone is up here, might as well come on out so there are no accidents," David's father said. "I don't want to have to shoot anyone."

I couldn't reach the phone cord.

"Rrrrgghh!" I said in total frustration.

I jumped up, glanced at the screen, dropped to my knees, and rolled under the bed.

From beneath the bed I saw shoes stepping slowly through David's door.

I held my breath.

And that's when I realized two really terrible things.

One: in my quick glance at David's monitor, I had noticed something odd. The clock in the lower, right-hand corner was wrong. It was off by an hour.

David's E-mail was going out not in an hour and three minutes, but in three minutes.

Two: David's pet cobra slept under the bed.

Chapter 11

It slithered up, over the lip of a cardboard box. And let me tell you something: time really is relative, because I aged about five years in five seconds.

It formed itself into a coil. And then, quite suddenly, up it went! Head flared wide, tongue flickering, it raised up and. . .

Bonk!

The cobra hit its head on the bottom of the mattress.

This seemed to leave it feeling puzzled, because it sort of hung there, half up, half down, staring at me like it was all my fault.

I remembered David saying it had been de-poisoned. Or what ever they call it. But how can you trust a kid who'd own a snake?

The snake stared at me with glittering, evil eyes.

The shoes came closer.

What was I supposed to do? I could morph to something small. Like a bug. Like a roach or an ant or a flea. But there was a slight problem with that: I was being eyeballed by a cobra not a metre away! Who knew what snakes might eat?

Then it hit me. The obvious, if slightly insane solution.

I reached my hand for the snake.

Fwapp!

The snake struck! Fangs in my hand, right in the fleshy part between the thumb and forefinger.

"Urgh!" I groaned.

"All right, come out from under there!" David's father said.

I grabbed for the snake and held him tight this time. He began to thrash, slither, wriggle, and just generally be annoying.

"On the count of three, and bring your hands out first!"

Thump!

A muffled noise. I saw the black shoes swivel to face the cupboard. It was Ax, providing a distraction. Good old Ax!

I held on to that stupid snake and I focused. When animals are acquired, which is when we

54

absorb their DNA, they become calm, relaxed, peaceful. Most of the time, anyway.

But not the snake. No, as I absorbed the DNA and as David's father went to the cupboard, that lunatic snake kept thrashing like an idiot.

The cupboard door opened.

"All right, step out here and . . . jeez Louise!"

I heard the sound of a gun being holstered. And then the big black shoes started doing a dance. A little dance called "stomp the bug"!

<Marco! I am in spider morph and this human is attempting to crush me with his artificial hooves!>

I couldn't answer, of course, since I wasn't in morph. All I could do was try to distract David's dad for Ax, like he'd done for me.

So I yanked the cobra back and flung him across the floor. He went flopping and hissing out into plain view. At which point David's father said, "Ah, Spawn! Get the spider, Spawn!"

Things were going from bad to worse. The cobra locked its nasty gaze right on poor Ax, who I could now see zipping around insanely between the man's big, black "artificial hooves".

Ax was going to get stomped or eaten, one or the other or possibly both.

Nothing to do now but crawl out from under the bed and. . .

Dingdong!

"Get that spider, Spawn! That's the door. Probably rent-a-cops from the security company, the useless . . . I told 'em not to bother." He muttered his way out of the room.

I squirmed quickly out from beneath the bed, stood up, narrowly missed stomping Ax myself, and pushed Spawn the snake out of the way.

I swept Ax up in my hand and leaped back to the computer.

And there, on the screen, the fateful words: Your mail has been sent.

I took a deep breath. I had a morphed Andalite in my hand. A deadly E-mail was on its way. David's policeman father could decide to come back up and resume his search. And I had a painful snake bite on my hand.

At least there was no poison. Or I'd probably be dead by now.

Unless it was one of those slow-acting poisons.

From downstairs I heard, "Hey, look, I told your office I didn't need them to send you. Waste of your time. Probably just a false alarm. I have it under control."

I guess he hadn't seen all the stuff Ax had accidentally broken.

The sound of the door shutting.

Now what? I wondered.

The E-mail had gone out. David's dad was

going to start searching again. And I didn't really want to leave the house. Trouble could start at any minute.

Spawn, the snake, had slithered away into the cupboard. No time for Ax to demorph and then remorph. There was maybe just enough time for one morph.

Just time for one morph that could stay right here in the room and not be noticed. Or eaten.

"Ax! I'm gonna morph! I'm putting you down."

I tossed Ax on to the floor. I wasn't too worried about dropping him. He was in wolf spider morph and I'd done that morph before. They're tough little creatures.

I focused my mind and began to morph.

I began to morph the cobra.

Chapter 12

Here's a news flash about snakes: they don't have arms or legs.

I began the morph and the first thing I noticed was that my arms and legs were withering. Not just shrinking. Withering. Like if you took a strip of paper and put it at the edge of a fire in the fireplace. And it doesn't quite burn, it just sort of . . . withers.

That was happening to my arms. It was bizarre. It was the kind of thing that would make any sane human being scream like a ninny. I mean, come on! You're looking at your arms and they have skin and muscles and hair, fingers on the end, fingernails, and all of that seems to crumple and weaken and shorten and shrivel.

But as bad as that is, your legs are worse. You need them for standing.

As soon as I realized what was happening I dropped to my knees. As quietly as I could, but I'm sure I still made some sound. Great! Now David's dad would definitely be coming back.

I rolled on to my side and back under the bed.

I twisted my head and realized that I was twisting it too well. My neck had grown. I could look straight down without crimping my neck.

What I saw was my morphing suit and my skin both begin to be covered by a pattern. Like tiny, tiny diamonds drawn in my flesh. The scales of the snake. They were yellow and a sort of dirty brown.

My arms were little twigs poking out from the trunk of my body. My legs were thinning and stretching, all muscle gone, my feet gone.

I heard the eerie sound of my own bones turning watery and disappearing. I literally felt the sagging of my internal organs as they sort of lay there, unsupported by the usual bone and muscle.

I could hear a faint "scrrrrrnnnnnnchhhh" as my spine extended out, forcing its way down one of my withered legs. And then, all at once, the other leg whipped around like a fast-action ivy or something. It whipped around the leg with my spine in it and melted together to form a tail.

Now, here's the gross part. Morphing, like I said before, is never logical. Things don't happen smoothly. Sometimes it's like they happen as weirdly as possible. Like the Andalite scientists who invented morphing had a twisted sense of humour or something.

Because even as the scales spread across my almost totally tubular body, and my legs became a tail, and my arms . . . well, they were gone now . . . but even while all this was happening, my head was untouched.

I know I still had my normal, human head. Normal size . . . with a snake where the rest of my body should be.

Yeah, get a good, clear mental picture of that. Think about it being you. And then think about just how much you'd want to scream right about then.

I was a worm with a head.

I've had two legs. I've had four legs. I've had six and eight legs. I've never had zero legs. Zero legs, zero arms.

Fortunately, my lungs were tiny snake lungs and couldn't have forced a sigh up through my human mouth, let alone a scream.

I am so going to have nightmares about this, I thought.

Then, at last, my head began to change. It was a relief. I mean, either be human or be a snake. Don't be a little of both.

You feel weird stuff during morphing. Never any pain, which is good, because seriously, you don't want to think about how much it would hurt to have half your internal organs disappear and have your spine shoving into new places where it doesn't belong.

But you sometimes feel things like they're far off. The way you feel things in a dream. Like they're happening to someone else, but they're still happening, right?

I could feel my windpipe, the part that goes to your mouth, push up, up through the roof of my mouth. Then I could feel it join with my nose. I have no idea why. All I know is, I couldn't breathe through my mouth any more.

My head was shrinking very fast now. The scales covered my neck, spreading up my cheeks like really bad acne, then across my forehead and over my scalp, replacing my hair.

My mouth was getting bigger, relative to my head. A normal human mouth is maybe, what, five per cent the size of the whole head? Well, now my mouth was about a third of my head.

I felt my teeth suddenly turn mushy. They became puffy flesh, like rotten gums.

And then I heard the sound of something growing inside my mouth. I felt it, too.

Fangs!

They grew and curled back up against the

61

roof of my mouth. Of course, Spawn had had his poison sacs removed. So. . .

Then it occurred to me: this morph was created from DNA. Surgery wouldn't affect that. The fact that Spawn had no poison did not mean I didn't.

I had fangs. Hollow needle teeth. And above those fangs, up in my mouth, poison filled the sacs.

Between those fangs my forked tongue whipped . . . out, tweedle-tweedle-tweedle as it wiggled. In. Out and tweedle, tweedle, tweedle. In.

It was like smell. Only not. I was tasting the air. But tasting it with more refinement than the world's greatest food lover. I was tasting individual molecules.

My sight was excellent. It was even in colour, which was a relief. Different colours from normal, but colour.

In addition, I felt a new sense, a new awareness added to the others. It took a while to figure out. But then I realized: I could sense heat. Not like the difference between a hot cooker and a block of ice. This was infinitely more refined. I could sense the difference in heat between the side of a carpet strand that was towards the faint sunlight, and the side that was in shadow.

The only real problem was hearing. Snakes

don't have external ears, you know. Mostly I was hearing through vibrations in the floor that seemed to travel up my body.

But then, I'm used to that. It's pretty much the same as when you're in cockroach morph.

Mostly, though, I was a creature of sight, with that questing, tasting tongue to back me up and an eerily precise ability to sense minuscule differences in temperature.

And that's when the snake's own mind appeared within my consciousness.

Cold.

That's how it felt. Like a ghost was standing beside me. Like someone had opened a door in my brain and a rush of Arctic air had blown in.

The snake heard the sound of footsteps approaching, climbing the stairs. It was wary. Not afraid, just . . . ready. Like Clint Eastwood walking into a saloon. Not afraid . . . just making sure his gun hand was free.

Tongue out, tweedle, tweedle, tweedle. Tongue in.

Wary and hungry.

I sensed heat. Not much, since what I was sensing was cold-blooded. But enough. The wide-set eyes spotted jerky movement, eight legs motoring.

<The human is coming again,> Ax said.

The cold, calculating, emotionless machine that was my brain noticed the odd sound in my head and dismissed it. Irrelevant. What mattered was hunger and movement and warmth.

Tongue out, tweedle, tweedle, tweedle. Hmmm. The musk of a bug. The scent of a spider. Movement, warmth and taste.

Movement and warmth and taste meant food. Food was the answer to hunger.

<Marco, what do you think we should do?> Ax asked.

I didn't answer. Instead, I reared up, cocked my head back, stretched the thin bones that spread my cobra cowl, and with speed as great as an Andalite's tail, I fired my head forward, mouth open.

I ate Ax.

I ate him in one quick swallow.

Chapter 13

I felt him squirming inside my mouth. I felt the eight hairy legs kicking.

<Did you ingest me?!> Ax demanded, sounding outraged.

<Um . . . yes.>

<Have you lost control of your morph?>

<Well. . .> OK, maybe I had. For just a minute. Now I was back in charge, though.

It was slightly embarrassing. As a rule, you shouldn't eat your friends.

Then something terrible occurred to me.

<Did I bite you? How do you feel?>

<Urgghh . . . groggy. . .>

<Morph out!> It didn't matter any more if David's father saw Ax. Ax would be dead in seconds if he didn't demorph.

I spat the spider out, which was not an easy thing to do. My snake tongue didn't work like a normal tongue. It came flitting out of its own little slot, tasting the air every second or so. It was great for picking up the scent of possible prey. It was useless for pushing half-dead spiders out of your mouth.

Fortunately, Ax was already demorphing. He was growing bigger and bigger in my snake mouth and pushing his own way out.

And that's when David's father reappeared.

"What the . . . Oh, oh, oh! What is that thing?"

No choice. I had to contact the man. I had to use thought-speak. Of course, there was no law saying I had to tell the truth. And it's a fact that you can't tell where thought-speak is coming from.

<Greetings, Earthling! *Klaatu barada nikto!* I come in peace!>

"Yaa-ah-ahh!" David's father said and backed up a couple of steps.

I saw him draw his weapon from a shoulder holster and point it at Ax. I couldn't blame him. Ax was about the size of a Beanie Baby, with eight hairy legs, blue and brown fur, a wormy sort of scorpion tail, and two very tiny arms.

<Do not fire your Earth weapon!> I yelled. <We come in peace!>

"'We'? A second ago it was 'I'. How many of you are there?"

66

Great. Count on a "law enforcement officer" to notice that. I recalled David saying his dad was a spy. What was he, FBI? CIA? Or a member of the shadowy secret force that's always giving Mulder and Scully so much trouble?

<Um, well, Earthling,> I said, <there's just one of me. But I suffer from a sort of space mental illness. Split personality. Hey, it's a long, long trip from planet Xenon Five, I had to have *someone* to talk to!>

Ax had grown to the size of a teddy bear. A really ugly teddy bear.

"What ever you're doing, stop it!" the man cried. "Stop growing!"

<Hey! What the heck are you two doing in there?>

It was Tobias's voice from outside.

<I'm a snake, I bit Ax, he's demorphing so he won't die of the poison, the stupid E-mail got sent, and this guy is gonna shoot us!> I said. <Any other questions?>

"Stop growing, or I'll shoot!" the man said.

Click!

He pulled back the hammer on the gun.

"I said freeze."

<You got new problems,> Tobias announced. <David's walking up.>

<Earthling!> I yelled. <Your son ditched school early!>

Don't ask me why I said that. I guess I had

67

some instinct that maybe all parents are alike and even when faced with a weird, morphing alien, they'll focus on their kids first.

The FBI slash CIA slash Secret Whatever Agency agent's eyes flickered. "He *what*?"

<He ditched last period.>

Now, let me step back and paint this picture for you: it's me, the snake, thought-speaking to a very suspicious guy, pretending to be speaking from a now cocker-spaniel-sized half-spider, half-Andalite, while getting information from a Bird-boy, announcing that some kid had ditched school early.

Question: is my life insane?

Answer: oh, yeah. Definitely.

"I came home from work early," David's father said. "Hah! Got him! I'll ground him for a month!"

The sound vibrations of a door opening downstairs.

Ax was now more Andalite than spider. And he was morphing his way clear of the poison.

"I told you to stop that," David's father said, snapping back to the fact that maybe, just *maybe*, having an alien in his house was slightly more important than catching his son skipping a class.

<Marco, hang in there,> Tobias reported from outside. <I see an eagle, an osprey and a falcon heading this way. Should be here in

about ten minutes.>

<That's great, as long as this guy doesn't decide to pull the trigger! 'Cause I'm guessing the bullet will take less than ten minutes to travel.>

David suddenly appeared in the doorway. He stopped dead and stared at Ax.

"Whoa!"

"He says he's some kind of alien," his father said tersely.

"Whoa-oah-oah!"

"By the way, you're grounded."

"An alien, no way!"

I'm sorry, I couldn't help myself. In thought-speak I said, <Yes, way!>

It would have all been stupidly funny. I mean, it was bizarre, that's for sure. But the humour vanished in the next instant.

Because that's when Tobias said, <A limo, two Jeeps and a removal van, coming fast, all together! Coming this way!>

And I said to David and his father, in as calm a voice as I could manage, <Listen to me. All hell is about to break loose. The two of you need to hide.>

"Hide? Why do we have to hide?" David said defiantly.

<Because the alternative is to be dead.>

Chapter 14

Dingdong!

The doorbell rang.

David's father kept the gun on Ax, who was now definitely an Andalite.

<You don't want to answer that doorbell,> I said.

Unfortunately, the real Spawn, the original cobra, chose that moment to slither out of the cupboard.

Slowly, David's father turned his gaze down to me. Then back to Ax, then to me again.

<Yes, it's me, the snake talking. Look, don't do anything stupid.>

He jerked the gun towards me.

BLAM! BLAM!

I felt an impact. Not pain, just an impact. I

jerked my snake head and saw a hole the size of a penny in my body, just fifteen centimetres up from the far end. I was seeing carpet *through* my snake body.

Now David's father was taking more careful aim.

Fwapp! Ax swung his tail like a bullwhip! The gun went flying. So did a finger.

"Hey!" David cried.

"Ahhh!" his father yelled.

CRRRRUNCH!

Downstairs, the door exploded in splinters.

David's father clutched his injured hand.

<TOBIAS!> I yelled in thought-speak. <We're gonna need reinforcements!>

There was a severe, house-shaking pounding as many large feet ran up the stairs.

Two Hork-Bajir warriors leaped into the room, saw Ax, and cringed back.

And then, between them, stepped another Andalite. Older than Ax. And in some way you couldn't quite put your finger on, very, very different from Ax.

<Visser Three!> Ax sneered in hatred.

<We heard shots. We thought maybe we could help,> the Visser said mockingly.

"Get out of here!" David yelled.

<Get out of here?> Visser Three said. <Why, I'm disappointed. I just got your primitive E-mail and I rushed right over.>

"Y-y-you want to b-b-buy the blue box?"

<Oh, yes, definitely,> Visser Three said. <I do, I do. And I'm willing to pay anything. Let's see, what could I offer you for the box? I know!> He whipped his tail and pressed the blade against the throat of David's father. <I'll pay you with your father's life.>

<You aren't getting the box,> Ax said calmly, stepping forward to tail-range with the Visser.

<Then this human will be separated from his head. I understand that's usually fatal in humans.>

For a long moment, no one moved. Not Visser Three. Not Ax. Not David or his father. Not the two Hork-Bajir.

No one moved. Except me.

I was new in the morph. I hadn't really tried it out yet. And I had no idea how you're supposed to move if you don't have legs. But the snake's own brain knew.

I slithered. Long muscles in my body contracted, shortening one side of my body, forming a half-loop. Then, I uncoiled the half-loop to push my head forward.

I was silent. I was swift. But I was not invisible. And I was losing blood from the bullet hole in my tail.

<What is this? Another Andalite in morph?> Visser Three wondered, cocking a stalk eye down at me.

Sudden movement!

David's father jerked his head back, away from the Visser's tail blade.

David ran straight at the Visser, yelling, "Let him go!"

Ax whipped his tail forward. Fwapp! But his attack was slowed by having to be careful of David.

Fwapp! The Visser blocked Ax's blow!

The two Hork-Bajir stopped looking like statues and leaped forward, blades flashing.

Two Hork-Bajir and Visser Three versus Ax and a snake. It was impossible! Doubly impossible with David and his father running round getting in the way.

Fwapp!

Fwapp!

Tail blades sliced the air.

Shwoop! Shwoop! Hork-Bajir wrist and arm blades slashed.

Ax was quickly driven back, desperate, against the far wall. It was a slashing, tail-whipping madness that ripped posters from the walls and lacerated curtains and sent all the little toys and bits on David's desk flying.

I slithered after him, coiling, stretching, coiling, sliding across the floor in pursuit of hooves and the big Hork-Bajir, Tyrannosaurus feet.

Target! A Hork-Bajir ankle!

I reared up, I sighted, I fired!

Fast as an Andalite tail, I launched my diamond head forward through the air, mouth open, fangs down.

Thmph!

Yes! I hit flesh! I sank my needle fangs in, all the way. I felt the venom pumping, pumping, pumping chemical death into the Hork-Bajir's leg.

"Rrrraahhhh!" the Hork-Bajir yelled in pain. He kicked, and I was like the end of a whip! He kicked madly, trying to dislodge me, but I was stuck to him by my fangs.

Back and forth! Whipped forward, whipped back. My head was almost still, glued to the vile Hork-Bajir leg, but the rest of my long body flailed away through the air.

Flail forward! <Aaaahhhh!>

Flail back! <Aaaahhhh!>

And then the Hork-Bajir began to slow down.

BLAM! BLAM! BLAM!

David's father had found his gun. He was in the corner, still cradling his bloody gun hand and firing with the other hand.

I saw three circles appear in my Hork-Bajir's chest and down he went.

I disengaged my teeth.

More Hork-Bajir rushing into the cramped room. I remembered Tobias saying a removal van was coming. That would hold a lot of Hork-

Bajir.

One big Hork-Bajir stepped on me, not even noticing I was there. A big mistake on his part. I jerked my head forward, quicker than the blink of an eye. This time I bit and released quickly.

Ax was down!

I saw him topple over and I saw Visser Three and two Hork-Bajir close in on him.

And that's when things got really ugly.

"Hhhhrrroooarrrhh!" There was a throaty, hoarse-sounding roar and through the door stepped something even more awesome, more terrifying than a Hork-Bajir warrior. Through the door, bowing her massive head and crunching her huge bulk, came Rachel.

If you were to come across a grizzly bear in the wild, out among the trees, it would look huge. But here, confined inside a bedroom, it was beyond huge. The bear was reared up on its hind legs and its cute little ears were scraping the ceiling. I mean, it scared me, and I knew it was just Rachel in a morph.

You want to know what it's like being a human up against a grizzly bear? Well, you know that "da,da,da,da" commercial for Volkswagen? Anyway, take that Volkswagen and run it head-to-head into an eighteen-wheeler going a hundred and fifty kilometres an hour. That's human versus grizzly.

You just have no concept, no concept at all,

of how powerful a grizzly bear is until you're up close and personal with it.

Hork-Bajir are nasty, tough opponents. But even they did a quick double take when Rachel stepped into the room. And behind her, sliding past her with unnatural grace, like molten steel, came a tiger.

The fight had been rowdy. Now it was going nuclear.

David was going to have a real problem cleaning up his room.

Chapter 15

David's room started out with the usual four walls.

Within seconds, it had only two.

It was an explosion of wild, insane violence.

A bunch of Hork-Bajir, a grizzly, two humans, a tiger, a real Andalite, an Andalite-Controller, and me, Snake-boy.

SLASH!

ROAR!

<Andalite scum!> Visser Three cried, enraged.

The bed ripped apart. Foam rubber protruded from the gash.

SLASH!

FWAPP!

<This time you won't escape, Visser,> Ax said bravely.

77

Rachel swung one ham-sized paw, hit a Hork-Bajir warrior, and knocked him through the wall. Not *into* the wall. *Through* the wall.

<About time you guys showed up!> I said. <We were getting our butts kicked.>

<Is there some reason why you're a snake?> Jake asked.

<Long story,> I said.

Crash! Some*one* or some*thing* went out the window.

I slithered forward, under the feet of the Hork-Bajir. I was looking for Andalite hooves. I was looking for Visser Three. I was going to drain my venom sacs into him.

But down there on the ground, looking up at all these monstrously tall creatures screaming and roaring and slashing and stomping, it wasn't easy.

Suddenly, Jake cut loose. Rachel's grizzly might be scarier to see, but Jake's tiger was amazing to hear.

RRRRROOOOOOOOOOWWWWWRRRR!

I mean, the floor jumped from the sound waves. The windows rattled. You could feel the air vibrating.

Then, hooves! Delicate, Andalite hooves. But whose? Ax? Or Visser Three?

As I stared through snake's eyes, I saw the hoof changing. Melting. And now growing.

It was Visser Three morphing!

I reared back. I flexed the bones that flared my hood. And I—

A hand reached down and grabbed me behind the neck. It was David.

"Look out, Spawn!" he cried.

<You idiot, put me down!> I roared in thought-speak.

David jumped back, startled, and dropped me. I spun, looking to take my shot. But then—

WHUMPF!

A big Hork-Bajir foot came down on me.

It didn't kill me, but it sure slowed me down. I lay there stunned, gazing up at Visser Three as he morphed.

Visser Three has morphs acquired from dozens of planets and moons spread all across the galaxy. We'd seen some of them. I had never seen this one.

It was as purple as Barney the Dinosaur. But it was not cute. And it didn't look to me like an animal that would sing "I love you, you love me". This purple monster did not have a happy family.

It rose from the body of Visser Three, hunched over beneath the ceiling. It had massive shoulders. Massive enough to make Rachel's grizzly shoulders look puny. It stood on two widely separated feet, each with four thick toes as big around as my thighs.

Its face . . . if you could call it a face . . .

was in the centre of its upper body, so it couldn't turn and look behind itself, only straight forward. Two big eyes blinked from where a guy's chest would be. Weird? Oh, yeah. Definitely weird.

As I watched in horror, the mouth grew, splitting open, a red-rimmed gash across the creature's belly. Serrated teeth and a tongue that lolled out almost like my own snake tongue.

And all of that was bad. But it wasn't as bad as what came next. Because from the shoulders grew four arms, two on each side. The arms started off smooth and muscular at the shoulder. But they became increasingly wrinkly as they went down towards the place where the hands should be. And instead of hands there were bony, deep, deep red points. They looked like, like, I don't know, like really sharp traffic cones. You know those things they put up on the motorway to divert traffic? That's what they looked like: sharp cones on the end of the four arms.

The two sides had separated a little: Rachel, Jake and Ax on one side, bloody, sweaty, gasping, hurt and mad. And the Hork-Bajir and Visser Three on the other side of the room. Between the two sides were the utterly destroyed remnants of David's bed.

Two of the walls were essentially gone. One wall now opened into a bathroom. David and his father were in there. David's father had his gun, but he was looking wildly from one of us to the other, probably wondering where to shoot. Who were the good guys?

The other battered wall opened on to the master bedroom. Twisted, shattered planks stuck out here and there. Slabs of breeze block were all askew.

I wondered where Tobias and Cassie were. But then I realized I could hear a whole other battle taking place downstairs. They were covering our rear.

Visser Three had completed his morph.

<It's called a *Dule Fansa*,> he said. <A rather fanciful name, don't you think? Would you like to see what it can do?>

He aimed one traffic cone hand at Ax.

FwoooooOOOMPH!

It shot out like a rocket. The wrinkled skin at the bottom of the arm extended, stretched, zoomed right out! The cone shot towards Ax. Ax dodged but caught a glancing blow that knocked him to his knees. The cone shot right on past Ax, into the one remaining wall, and punched a metre hole through it.

In the blink of an eye, the cone hand retracted and wrinkled up, ready to fire again.

<Now, let's make this simple,> Visser Three said confidently. <I want the blue box. I will have the blue box. Or all of you will die.>

Chapter 16

Fact One: there was no way we could let Visser Three have that box.

Fact Two: I didn't even know where the box was.

Fact Three: there were now six Hork-Bajir crammed into the room and the adjoining master bedroom. Plus Visser Three in his powerful morph. More Hork-Bajir downstairs were keeping Cassie and Tobias from helping us.

So Fact Four was: we were not going to win this fight.

<We need to bail,> I said to Jake and Rachel.

<We can't. If we leave, the Yeerks can tear this place apart and find the box,> Jake pointed out.

<Where is the stupid box?> Rachel wondered.

I should point out that thought-speak is a little like E-mail. It's only heard by the people you want it to be heard by. Unless you're speaking "in the open", in which case it's like any normal voice and can be heard by anyone within range.

The three of us were talking only to each other. But when the Visser spoke it was for all to hear.

<I'm not a patient Yeerk,> Visser Three said. <I'll have the blue box. And I'll destroy you all. But if I get the blue box now, I may decide to destroy you some other time.>

<Only David knows where the box is,> I pointed out.

<OK,> Jake said. <Ask him.>

<David,> I said, directing my thought-speak to him. <David, listen to me.>

I saw his frightened eyes darting, looking for the source of the voice. He was in the bathtub. Not a bad place to be, considering the other choices.

<David, listen to me. I'm on your side. We have to rescue that box. So we have to know where it is.>

Visser Three glared at Ax with his chest-mounted eyes. <Brave Andalites,> he mocked. <You'll let me kill these humans rather than give up the box?>

"No!" David shouted suddenly. "I have the stupid box. Just let us go. I have the stupid box right here in my backpack, if you want it so bad."

He started to unsling his backpack. And about ten other things happened at once. The Hork-Bajir leaped for him.

His father fired. BLAM! BLAM! BLAM! CLICK. . .

Ax whipped his tail towards the Visser's morph.

Rachel muscled forward, trying to grab David or his backpack or both.

The Visser took Ax's tail blade on one pile-driver arm. "Aarrraaawwwggghh!" the Visser screamed as Ax's blade sliced neatly through one arm.

Jake coiled his powerful legs and leaped straight at the Visser, ignoring the Hork-Bajir.

I struck the closest Hork-Bajir leg I could find and emptied my poison sacs into him.

<Rachel! Get that kid outta here!> Jake yelled.

Rachel bellowed, lowered her head, landed on all fours and ran straight at David. Like a train. Like a Mack truck she ran. Straight at him.

Hork-Bajir slashed at her. I shot a glance and saw what she was doing. There was a small bathroom window. She was going to try to shove him through it. Not exactly fun for David, getting rammed through glass and dropped from the second storey, but David's alternatives weren't too good.

Rachel ran.

David cowered.

And the Visser fired two massive pile-driver cone hands straight for David.

WHUM-WHUMPH! WHAM! CRUNCH!

The cone hands missed and blew a hole in the outer wall of David's bathroom. In a flash he was swept up by a mountain of bear, shoved through the shattered plaster and glass, and propelled out into the late afternoon air.

I knew Visser Three could not afford to go racing around a whole block in his alien morph, followed by a dozen Hork-Bajir warriors. But I also knew he was going to take it out on someone. And the someones were me, Ax and Jake.

WHAM! The pile-driver fist fired at Jake. I felt the breeze from it as it shot past my face. It hit Jake in the flank. He went down hard.

WHAM! The left side fired at Ax. Ax dodged, but just barely. He staggered aside and almost fell through the hole. He was off-balance, teetering. He couldn't hold on, so he turned it into a jump. By the time he hit the ground outside, he was already morphing out of his Andalite body.

<Jake, run!> I yelled.

He ran. But his back legs were dragging.

The Hork-Bajir encircled him, slashing, hacking, attacking. And I was helpless!

Then, swift, silent, unexpected, a flash of grey and white burst into the room. A wolf, running low to the ground, teeth bared. Cassie!

She leaped straight on to the back of the closest Hork-Bajir and locked her jaws on the back of his neck.

Jake staggered the last metre or so to the hole in the wall and half-jumped, half-fell through it, to land hard and painfully on the grass below.

Cassie unclamped her jaws and used the back of the Hork-Bajir to simply spring over him, sail through the wall, and drop gracefully to the ground below.

Everyone was out. Everyone but me and David's father. Two Hork-Bajir had him by the arms. He was yelling. He was crying his son's name, over and over.

"David! David! David!"

I was still there. Visser Three's awful gaze focused on me.

I slithered under the bed, fast as I could. I raised up into strike position, hooked myself over one of the bed slats, and held on, wishing I were a python.

Powerful hands threw the bed back.

<Hah-hah! We'll have one Andalite to play with, at least!> Visser Three gloated.

But what they saw on the floor was not me. It was Spawn.

The Hork-Bajir threw a towel over Spawn and gathered him up. They stomped away, down the stairs, carrying what they thought was an Andalite in morph.

I didn't want to think what they'd do to the poor snake. Maybe just hold him, waiting for him to demorph.

But maybe when they realized that wasn't happening, they'd do other things. Visser Three is an evil, vengeful creature.

As for David's father . . . he'd seen too much. There was only one fate for him: within hours he'd have a Yeerk slug inside his brain.

His life as a free human being was over.

Visser Three stayed behind for a moment, after his Hork-Bajir and their prisoners were gone. Did he sense something wrong? Did he sense that I was still there? I was in plain sight, curled tightly around the upturned bed slat.

I froze. I was so still I could have been dead.

Visser Three demorphed. Back to his stolen Andalite body.

He took one last look around the room.

I wished he'd come closer. Maybe my poison sacs were full again. Maybe I had enough to destroy him.

87

But he didn't come within range. He morphed into his human form and walked calmly from the room.

Chapter 17

Police rushed to the scene. We heard their sirens as we were escaping and demorphing. But by the time they got there, my friends were gone. So were the Yeerks.

David's house was practically a hollowed-out shell.

I demorphed to human, then to osprey, and I flew away just as the police came rushing inside.

I spotted my friends down below. They had all demorphed, except for Ax, of course, who had morphed his human form.

They were man-handling David along between them. He was unconscious. I didn't know if the fall had knocked him out or what.

I swooped down and landed in a dump-bin in

an alleyway. I demorphed there, away from prying eyes, and climbed out. The others were just reaching the alley.

"Hey," I said, catching their attention. Jake hustled the still-groggy-but-reviving David into the alley.

Rachel and I helped place David gently against the greasy brick wall.

"They took his dad," I said.

<They took his mum, too,> Tobias said, swooping down silently to land on the lip of the dump-bin. <I stayed over the house till everyone was clear. David's mum pulled up just as the Yeerks were pulling out. A Hork-Bajir snatched her up.>

"She'll be a Controller next time anyone sees her," Rachel said. She looked down at David. "Poor kid."

"He has no one to go home to," Cassie said. "Visser Three knows his name, his face, his address. By now he knows what classes he's in at school and where he hangs out. He's marked. If we let him go they'll take him, too. They'll make him a Controller."

I nodded. Then I reached into his backpack and fumbled around till I felt the smooth, hard edges. I withdrew my hand, holding the blue box.

"He hasn't seen any of us," I said. "He can't give us up to the Yeerks. They'll take him, make him a Controller, and he still won't be able to give us up."

<What do you want to do, Marco?> Tobias asked. <Just write this kid off?>

"You have another idea?" I said.

"Harsh," Rachel commented. But I could see she agreed with me.

"There is perhaps one other alternative," Ax said. He was in his weirdly handsome/pretty human morph. He'd created the morph by taking DNA from Jake, Rachel, Cassie and me. To this day it's weird, looking at him and seeing elements of myself joined with elements of Rachel, Cassie, or Jake.

"What alternative?" Jake asked Ax.

"We have the box," Ax said. "Box. Box-uh. We could use it. The box-uh."

We all stared at him.

"Create a new Animorph?" I asked sceptically.

"Create a new Animorph!" Cassie said enthusiastically.

Jake was nodding. Rachel was thinking about it, looking from Cassie to Jake back to David, zoned out on the ground.

"I don't like it," Rachel said.

"The question is, do we have any alternative?" Jake argued. "I mean, look, the kid is gonna wake up. I can't keep him knocked out. So it's down to this: we either make him one of us, or we leave him, right here, right now. In this alleyway. With parents who will be Controllers soon. With Visser Three knowing his name and looking for the blue box."

"It's harsh," I said, "but I don't see this guy fitting in with us. We don't know him."

<We didn't all know each other back when Elfangor used the box on us,> Tobias pointed out.

"We didn't know *you*, Tobias," Rachel said. "But Cassie and I were already best friends. Cassie and Jake were, um . . . friends. Jake was my cousin. Marco was his best friend. There were connections. Aside from you. And Ax. With this David guy, no connections."

It's weird, somehow, the way Rachel and I often end up on the same side. She likes Tobias more than me, and Cassie a lot more than me, but it's often the two of us together on big issues.

"Big risk," Jake said thoughtfully. "If he works out, we're stronger. If he doesn't . . ."

"Look, we have the box, right?" Cassie said. "The point is, maybe David here is just the first of many. I mean, we can use the box to create more and more Animorphs. Dozens. Hundreds. The more of us there are, the more we can hurt the Yeerks."

That was a pretty good point. I hadn't thought of that. But she was right. It wasn't just about this one kid. It was about a long-term strategy.

Rachel looked at me. "If you're in a war, you want more troops rather than less, right? Makes sense. Besides, we could be a little less cautious that way. With just us six we have to be careful."

I could feel a rush of excitement at the idea. I mean, Rachel was right, too. We had to be so careful now. We couldn't afford to take some risks. With more Animorphs, we could try to let the whole world know what was happening. We could infiltrate the Letterman show and morph on-stage and make people realize what we were saying was true. Or go to the President and show him our powers and then he'd have to listen to us.

We could actually win the war, instead of just maintaining.

And yet. . .

I spread my hands, pleading. "He names his cat Megadeth. He has a cobra named Spawn. What kind of a kid is that?"

Cassie shrugged. "A kid with bad taste in music and good taste in comic books?"

<I don't see we have a choice,> Tobias said. <But it's Jake's call.>

"Yes, Prince Jake should decide," Ax agreed.

"This is a big step," Jake said, shaking his head firmly. "If Erek is right, and he usually is, we are coming up against the toughest mission ever. The most important mission ever. I'm not going to make this decision on my own. Not this time. We do this by vote. Simple question: do we make David one of us, yes or no?"

<Yes,> Tobias said. <Can't just leave him to Visser Three.>

"I vote yes," Cassie said. "We have to make a leap of faith here and hope it will work out."

I snorted. I can't help it. It's my automatic reaction any time people start talking about "leaps of faith". Cassie smiled tolerantly at me.

"I should not vote," Ax said. "I follow Prince Jake. Jay-kuh."

Jake shook his head. "Nope. You are a part of the group, Ax. In battle, maybe there isn't time to vote on everything, but this is a democracy."

"Then I vote no," Ax said.

My eyebrows shot up. There were six of us altogether. This vote could still go my way.

<Just out of curiosity, why, Ax-man?> Tobias asked.

"We are not an army. We are a guerrilla group," he said. "Guerrilla, gorilla? The differences between the two words are very subtle. You humans should not make your words so. . . But my point is, going from six members to seven will not make us much stronger, and it carries risk. Risssss-kuh."

"If we're talking about having hundreds, maybe thousands of Animorphs eventually, don't we have to start somewhere?" Cassie asked.

"Yes," Ax agreed. "But we should start with someone we understand. Not a stranger. We have this mission before us, to save the human leaders of your various countries. A seventh person might help us. But it might also make our team indecisive, uncertain."

Jake looked at me.

"I'm with Ax," I said. "Something about this guy doesn't feel right to me."

"Two in favour, two against," Jake summarized. "Rachel?"

Rachel would vote against. Then, even if Jake was for it, we'd have a tie. Jake would never go ahead if we had a tie vote. I was starting to feel relieved and guilty all at once. I didn't enjoy thinking about David's fate.

"Let's do it," Rachel said.

"What?" I yelped.

"You heard me," Rachel said. "Ax makes a good point. One extra member just adds risk. But Cassie's right, too. We have to start somewhere, now that we have the box. What are we going to do, run an ad in the newspaper? 'Help wanted: danger, nightmares, big-time creepiness, no pay? Have you ever wanted to turn into a bug and fight brain-stealing aliens? Well, call 1-800-ANIMORPH.'"

Cassie laughed. "The sad thing is, Rachel, *you* would actually respond to an ad like that."

Rachel laughed. "Exactly. So you see the kind of people we'd get."

It was up to Jake now.

David moaned and moved his head. His eyes fluttered open.

"Who are you?" he asked, blinking up at Jake, then looking round at the rest of us.

Jake sighed. "We're the people who are going to totally change your world, David."

Chapter 18

"They are called Yeerks," Jake said.

We were back in Cassie's barn, among the caged, wounded animals. Amidst the smells of hay, medicine and animal poop. David was sitting on a bale of hay, rubbing his jaw. We were standing round him.

"They are a parasitic race from another planet. They are not much more than grey slugs, really. But they enter your brain and reduce you to slavery. Those big, two-metre-tall creatures that were in your house? Those are Hork-Bajir. They have Yeerks in their brains. An entire species already enslaved by the Yeerks."

"And now they're after the human race," Cassie said. "There are thousands of humans who've been made into Controllers. That's what you call a creature who's controlled by a Yeerk."

"My brother is one," Jake said.

"And by now, David, so are your mother and your father," I said.

Cassie shot me an angry, disapproving look. Jake obviously agreed with her.

I shrugged. "He needs to know what's happening," I said. "He needs to know this isn't just some game."

"What about my mum and dad?" David asked me directly.

I sighed. "Look, it's all about that blue box you found. The Yeerks want it. The guy who turned into the big purple pile driver? That's Visser Three. He's the leader of the Yeerks here on Earth. He's running the invasion, OK? As you may have noticed, he wants the box. And he allowed your father, and your mum, too, I guess, to see the truth. To see *him*. And that's a no-no. The Yeerks don't want people knowing what's happening, not yet. So he's going to keep your mum and dad quiet. Plus, he's going to find out what they know about the box."

David shook his head, not understanding. "Are you saying he'll torture them or something?"

"Man," I muttered. Explaining everything was going to be hard. I walked over and stood right in front of David. "Listen to me. By now your parents have been taken to a secret, underground facility called a Yeerk pool. It's not a nice place. Picture a sludgy cesspool of a pond the colour of molten lead. There are two steel piers leading out over the pond. Hork-Bajir warriors will drag your parents out to the end of one of those piers. They will—"

"Marco!" Cassie said angrily.

"They will drag them out to the end of that pier and they will kick their legs out from under them and force their heads down into the sludge. And while they are kicking and screaming and calling for help, a Yeerk slug will swim over and it will squeeze into one ear. And it will flatten itself out and squeeze and burrow and dig its way into their skulls, where it will spread around and into their brains. And the Hork-Bajir will yank them up out of the sludge, and they will start to feel that they can not control their own arms or legs. Can not open their own mouths or move their own eyes. The Yeerk will open their memories like a person opening a book. They will be slaves. The most total slaves in all of history because even their own minds won't be theirs any more. Are you getting the picture?"

Throughout all this, David had just stared at me. But slowly, without me noticing at first, tears had begun to well up in his eyes, and now I jerked myself away. I was panting. Feeling like. . .

I could see it all happening in my imagination. As I'd been talking, it wasn't David's mother I was seeing, it was my own.

Silence in the barn. Even the animals seemed quiet.

"My mum is one," I said flatly. "She's a Controller."

"There's a lot to tell you, David," Jake said quietly. "But Marco's right. You need to know this isn't a game. This is life and death. This is the future of the whole human race. It's too late to help your parents. And as of now, you have no home and you can't go back to school. You do, they'll find you. And it'll be you taking that long walk down the steel pier."

I saw the expression in David's eyes darken further still. It's not every day someone tells you your life is over.

"This is stupid," David said. "I mean . . . it's not right. Can't be. This is all some kind of trick."

"You saw what went down at your house," Rachel said.

"That could have been guys dressed up in costumes," David argued.

"You saw Visser Three morph," Cassie pointed out.

"What's a Kisser Three?"

"Visser Three. With a 'v'," Jake said. "The one who looked like a deer with a scorpion tail.

100

You saw him morph into that purple pile-driver monster."

David looked sullen. "It's all a trick."

I shot a look at Rachel. She looked like she was already regretting her vote.

"Ax," Jake said. "Demorph."

Ax nodded his human head. "I would be glad to. It is very disturbing being without my tail. Diss-ter-BING."

"David, watch Ax. Watch him closely."

David stared as Ax began to change. Hooves began to grow on his feet. His arms became thinner and weaker. Extra fingers emerged on his hands. His lips were sealed together, and then faded to the colour of the surrounding skin, and finally disappeared altogether. His front legs began to emerge, growing straight out of his chest.

"Aaaahhh! Aaaahhh!" David cried. He jumped back, stumbled, and started to run.

Rachel grabbed him. "It's OK, you'll get used to it," she said. She turned him round and pushed him back towards the hay bale he'd been sitting on.

There was a slight slurping sound as Ax's tail began to appear. Ax fell forward on all fours. The stalks grew from the top of his head and then — pop! pop! — eyes appeared on the ends of the stalks.

"See?" Jake said. "No trick. This is Aximili-

Esgarrouth-Isthill. We call him 'Ax' for short. He's an Andalite. The Andalites are the good guys of the galaxy."

"Mostly, anyway," I muttered.

"Visser Three, who you saw in your room, has an Andalite body. But he's a Yeerk underneath it all. He has just stolen and enslaved an Andalite."

David was shaking. I don't know how much he was absorbing. I felt like laughing. I mean, it was insane, of course. This poor kid is minding his own business one minute, and suddenly he's in the middle of . . .

But come to think of it, that's just what had happened to all of us, back one night when we walked through an empty construction site.

Back then I hadn't even wanted anything to do with being an Animorph. Jake hadn't wanted to be a leader. Cassie had just wanted to hug trees and take care of her animals. Tobias was a lost, messed-up kid looking for someone to care about him. A *human* kid.

Rachel . . . well, I personally think Rachel was glad to see her life go this way. Rachel always was a warrior hiding inside a fashion queen.

How would David deal with it all? Would he resist, like I had? Would he embrace it like Rachel?

"There is one nice thing about all this,"

Cassie said. "There is a compensation for all the danger and all the fear."

David looked at her, uncomprehending.

"You know the wild animals who were fighting the Yeerks today? You know the birds who tried to steal the blue box before that?" I said. "Us. That was us. See, Visser Three and Ax aren't the only ones who can morph. So can we. And now that we have this," I lifted up the blue box, "so can you."

"Any animal you can touch, you can *become*," Cassie said. "A dolphin, a skunk, a wolf."

"An elephant or a grizzly bear," Rachel said.

"A gorilla. A shark," I said.

"A tiger, a fly, a cockroach," Jake said. "Any animal. Any size. But only for two hours at a time. You can never stay in morph for more than two hours."

"Why?" David wondered.

"Meet the final member of the Animorphs," I said. "David, my man, meet Tobias."

Chapter 19

David spent the night at my house. I told my dad it was a sleepover. I gave him my bed and I used my sleeping bag and an air mattress. An air mattress that had lost all its air by two A.M.

Which was a good thing, because I woke up when David was sneaking from the room. I found him starting to make a phone call from the hall phone.

I put my finger down on the buttons before he could dial. "Ever heard of Caller ID?" I whispered.

"I'm calling my mum and dad," he said fiercely.

I nodded. "OK. But not from here."

We got dressed and crept past my dad's room and down the stairs. It was chilly outside and damp.

"Come on," I said.

"Where are we going?"

"You want to call home, fine. We'll call. But from a callbox. And then we'll see what happens."

I led him down the street, hoping no cop would pass by and notice us. I wasn't used to roaming the streets late at night. At least not as a human. Normally, I'd be in morph.

I took him down the dark, quiet streets, out through the gate, and along the boulevard to the 7-Eleven. There was a phone on the street side of the 7-Eleven car park.

"OK, now listen up," I said to David. "We do this my way. You can call. Tell your parents you're all right. Don't tell them who you're *with*. Don't tell them where you *are*. Got it?"

He nodded. But I don't think he intended to listen to me. That was OK, because I wasn't going to leave him alone. My finger would be a centimetre from the little lever, ready to kill the phone call if I even thought he was about to say anything wrong.

David pumped in a coin and started to dial. I grabbed his arm. "Before you do that, let me tell you exactly what's going to happen. Your mum and dad will sound totally normal. They'll tell you to come home. If you refuse, they'll ask where you are. Ask them what happened today at the house. Just that."

David finished dialling.

"Hello? Dad? It's me. It's me."

I waited while he listened.

"No, I'm not OK, I'm scared."

Listening again.

I silently mouthed the words "ask him".

"Dad, what happened? I mean, those were aliens and all."

David listened. His eyes turned to me. I could see the dull fear.

"It was all a trick?" he echoed back. "It was guys from your work playing a trick?"

I rolled my eyes. I'd expected some lame lie, but that was really lame.

"Dad, I saw that one alien turn into something else. That was real."

Pause.

"I'm OK, I'm—"

Click! I stopped the call.

David turned on me, furious. He looked eerie in the neon and fluorescent glow from the 7-Eleven.

"What are you doing?" he demanded.

I grabbed his sleeve. "Come on. That's time enough."

He shook me off. "Step off, Marco, you don't tell me what to do."

"Listen, you idiot, in about two minutes a couple of carloads of Yeerks are going to come screaming up looking for you. They'll trace the

106

call."

"My dad wouldn't do that."

"No? Come with me. We can watch. We can see what happens."

He came with me across the street. There's a row of older buildings over there. The kind with deep, dark doorways. We slunk back into the shadows.

I was wrong. It didn't take two minutes.

Two Jeeps, windows darkened, came roaring down the street a minute and a half later. The long, sinister limousine was not far behind. Human-Controllers leaped from the Jeeps. No Hork-Bajir this time. Not out in the open.

"See?"

"That doesn't prove anything," David hissed.

But then another car came squealing up. David's father and mother jumped out. They joined the others.

His father began passing out photographs.

"Your picture," I said.

"They're guys from my dad's work," David said. "Other spies, like him."

"What *exactly* does your dad do for a living?"

"He works for the National Security Agency. So, see, he would be able to trace the call, and he'd have his work buds with him. He's just looking for me, that's all."

His father and two of the other men dodged traffic and ran across the boulevard. Others spread out into the store and around the back, looking here and there.

His father and the two men came down the pavement straight for us. We could hear their footsteps. We could hear his father's voice.

"If we don't find that kid, Visser Three will make us wish we were dead," David's father said.

I looked at David. I saw him sag. I was afraid he'd collapse.

"He's coming this way," David said, his voice cracking. "He'll see us."

<No, he won't,> I said in thought-speak.

I guess David didn't notice that he hadn't really heard my voice. His father and the other two came closer.

And then. . .

PAH-LUMP, PAH-LUMP, PAH-LUMP, PAH-LUMP.

There came the sound of something running. Something large.

I stuck my head out of the shadows to watch. David did the same. The three Controllers heard the heavy galloping sound and turned.

There, running down the pavement, came a rhinoceros.

David's father and one of the men were bright enough to get out of the way. The third man was not.

WHUMPF!

Rhino horn hit human flesh and human flesh didn't do so well. The Controller flew up, over, cartwheeled once, and landed hard on the pavement.

<That would be Jake,> I said calmly. <He and the others have been taking turns watching my house in case there was any trouble. They followed us.>

David's father turned, drew his gun, and aimed for Jake's retreating butt. Not that a little pistol was going to do serious damage to a rhino butt, still. . .

I stepped out, wrapped one massive gorilla hand around the back of David's father's neck, and tossed him lightly against the wall.

David's father hit, bounced, and fell to the ground with a sigh.

The other Controller took a long, gaping look at me. At my tree-trunk arms and bulldozer gorilla head and shoulders.

"It's a trap!" he yelled and scurried back across the boulevard.

<Seen enough?> I asked David.

Chapter 20

We moved David from my house to Jake's house. We didn't have any idea what to do with him long-term. He couldn't go home. He couldn't go anywhere. He was a hunted person. And we could not allow him to be caught. Not with what he knew.

The day after he witnessed his father as a Controller, we assembled in the woods. Cassie's dad was working in the barn. Even though it was still chilly outside and the sky was filled with clouds, we were tramping along, clutching our sweatshirts and jackets closed with one hand.

With the other hand we were carrying a large, divided wire cage. We'd passed poles through, front to back, one on each side. Cassie, Jake, Rachel and I each had a pole-end. David walked alongside, a little off by himself. Tobias and Ax were in the woods.

In the cages were two big birds of prey: a merlin and a golden eagle. The merlin was about a quarter of the size of the eagle. The eagle was one big bird. And heavy. My carrying arm was straining.

Both birds had been patients of Cassie and her dad. Both were going to be released.

Tobias came swooping down, seemingly out of the clouds. He landed with easy precision on a small log.

<What are you doing with *that*?> he demanded, glaring at the eagle.

"Relax, relax, Tobias," Cassie said, setting down the cage.

<You're not releasing him near my territory,> he said flatly.

"Tobias, this bird has only been at the clinic for a couple of days. He has a well-established territory well back in the mountains. You know golden eagles don't like roosting in trees if they can find a nice cliff. So he won't be hanging around. But we can't get him any closer to his territory, really, because the road back up there washed out."

Tobias stared fiercely at her. But then, Tobias always looks fierce. That hawk face never looks exactly happy or relaxed.

He switched his gaze to David, then to Jake.

It was a clear, unspoken question.

"David's here to acquire his first morph. The merlin."

"Which one's the merlin?" David asked.

"The smaller bird," Cassie said. "They're very fast, very agile," she added helpfully.

"Faster than the big one?" David asked.

<You don't want to be a golden eagle,> Tobias said. <They're jerks. They go after other birds. Not to mention anything from a rabbit to a small deer. And I'm not kidding about the deer. I saw a golden eagle take down a young doe. Sank those talons right into the back of her head, boom, she went down like she'd been shot.>

"I want to do the eagle," David said.

A moment's hesitation. "Any special reason?" Jake asked.

"Yeah. You tell me I have no home. No family. Now I'm supposed to be in the middle of some war with aliens. If I'm in a war, I want to kick butt."

Jake nodded. "It isn't always about sheer power. That golden eagle is as big as a bald eagle, and we have problems sometimes with Rachel being a bald eagle because of the size."

"That bird has a two-metre-plus wingspan," Cassie pointed out.

David nodded and looked down at the leaves and grass underfoot. "Did Jake here tell you all what animals to morph? Or did you pick them yourselves?"

"I'm not telling you what animal to morph," Jake said calmly. But it was that calm voice Jake uses when he's actually starting to get mad.

"OK, then I'll morph the eagle," David insisted.

"Here's an idea," I said. "How about not being such a jerk? We saved you from the Yeerks. We've been doing this for a while, all right? We know what we're talking about. And Jake is the leader of this little group, so how about if you show some respect?"

"Who are you, my father?" David sneered. "You don't tell me what to do. No one tells me what to do. As for saving me, hah! That's a joke. You wanted the blue box, and now you have it, and you know what I have? Nothing. That's what I have, nothing. So thanks."

I don't know what I'd expected from David. I couldn't be a hypocrite. I wasn't thrilled about being an Animorph at first, either. I didn't care about saving the world then. I just cared about my dad not getting hurt any more. And I guess I didn't really accept it all until I discovered my mother was a Controller. That's when I knew we had to fight.

"Look, kid—" Rachel began.

But Jake gave a little shake of his head and

113

Rachel stopped talking and just fumed.

"You guys all think you're so tough and so cool," David said. "All these battles you've been in and all. But now, here I am, the new guy — as usual for me — and you don't like me."

"No one doesn't like you," Cassie said.

David turned his head to stare right at me. "*He* doesn't. I'm not an idiot, you know. I can tell what people think about me. My family moves every couple of years whenever my dad gets transferred. I'm always the new kid in school. So I've got good at telling what people think of me. And now, here I am in this different school. And I'm the new kid." He shrugged. "So, look, maybe you like me, maybe you don't like me. I don't care. I'm here. If you use the blue box on me I'm one of you. But I'm not going to get pushed around. And I'm not going to be all, 'Oh, thank you, wise and wonderful Animorphs, for letting me join'. If I'm in, I'm in all the way. If not . . . I guess I'll walk away and try to figure out what to do. On my own."

The funny thing was, I kind of liked David's little speech. I like people who push back when they get pushed. I liked the speech. I liked the attitude. I still didn't like David.

But Rachel laughed out loud. "Oh, he'll fit in fine."

Jake looked at Tobias. "Where's Ax?"

<Can't you hear him? You people are so deaf.

He's galloping, should appear right about . . . there.>

Ax sprang lightly into view. <I am sorry to be late,> he said. <I had to go out of my way to avoid some human campers. Are we going ahead with the Escafil Device?>

Jake hesitated, just a split second before saying, "Yes."

Rachel had been carrying the blue box in a waist pouch. She unzipped the pouch, popped out the box, and tossed it to Ax. Ax missed the catch. Andalite hands are weak and slow. But before the box could hit the ground, Ax whipped his tail forward, turned the blade flat, and caught the box. He raised the box to his hands.

<Press your hand on the square nearest to you,> Ax said.

"Wait! Shouldn't there be some kind of ceremony or something?" Cassie said.

"Like what?" I asked. "You want us all to join hands and sing 'The Star-Spangled Banner'?"

"No, I don't know all the words," Cassie said. With a sly grin she added, "We could sing 'MMMBop'."

We all laughed. Even David.

Ax held out the cube in one hand. David stepped forward, still obviously a little intimidated by Ax. He pressed his hand down on the cube.

"It tingles," David said.

Suddenly I was back in that dark construction site. Back with Jake and Rachel and Cassie, with a human Tobias and a dying Elfangor.

I barely recognized the person I'd been back then. I had changed. Everything had changed that night.

Now David, another kid not very different from any of us, had been dragged into this nightmare reality of great power and greater fear.

Maybe I didn't like him. But I felt sorry for him.

I stepped up to him and stuck out my hand. He took it. "Welcome to the Animorphs, new boy."

We each shook his hand. And then Cassie cracked open the cage of the golden eagle.

"You just put your hand in very slowly," she instructed.

David's shaking hand moved towards the bird.

"Now press your palm against the bird's shoulder."

He did. The eagle gave him a dirty look, but then ignored him.

"Focus your mind. See the eagle in your imagination. Think about him, what he is, what he represents."

David's eyes fluttered shut.

"Now take your hand away," Cassie said

softly. "You now have the golden eagle inside you. His DNA is in your blood. You can *become* him."

David grinned. "When do I do it?"

"Soon," Jake said. "We also have to get you a morph with some teeth. Cassie? Take David to the zoo. With your access he should be able to get in and out without being spotted, but the rest of us will fly cover. Let him have what ever morph he wants. But also get him a bug or two in case he has to get small. We want to be ready," he said, switching back to David. "We have a little . . . situation. A mission."

"Nothing to worry about, though," I said. "Just the usual: save the world from the alien invaders. You'll get used to it."

Chapter 21

There were two big tests ahead for David. One was his first morphing. The other was his first battle.

We'd all got used to morphing. Almost. But the first time was a serious eye-opener. You think you've experienced weird? You haven't experienced anything until you watch your own body turn into something extremely different.

It would have been nice to have some time to prepare David. But there was no time. Erek had told us the world leaders would be showing up in four days. Time was up. They were coming. And we had to figure out which one was a Controller, protect the others, and if at all possible, find a way to warn them all of the Yeerk conspiracy.

"I have the brochure," Rachel announced as we met once again at Cassie's barn. "I downloaded it off the Internet."

She held out some colour printer pages showing the Marriott resort. There were photographs of rooms. Pictures of giddy, happy people in bathing suits, a shot of a big buffet table maybe fifteen metres long and loaded with food, and a map of the resort. The map showed a big, main hotel building that was twenty storeys high. And down, closer to the beach, a jumble of smaller "cottages". Ten cottages in all.

"They'll be in the cottages," I said. "The leaders, I mean. They'll dump all their people in the main hotel building."

"Sounds right," Jake agreed.

"They'll have security so tight no one will be able to burp without nine guys in sunglasses running over with their Uzis cocked and ready." I counted off on my fingers. "French security, German security, Japanese security—"

"Ninjas?" David asked.

"Yeah, Jackie Chan himself," I said, rolling my eyes.

"He's Chinese, not Japanese," David said, rolling his eyes back at me.

"British security," I said, adding quickly, "and no one say, 'Bond, James Bond', please. Russian security and American secret service, FBI, and local cops."

Jake sighed and shook his head.

"Now just to make things really fun," I continued, "there are the Yeerks. How many of the hotel's maids and waiters and pool boys are Controllers? Don't know. How many of the Russian, German, British, French, Japanese and US security guys are also Controllers? Don't know. All we know is that one of these presidents or prime ministers is a Controller."

"At least one," Cassie said. "Sorry to interrupt, but it's kind of important. Erek said one of them was a Controller. He didn't say for sure that the other five were not."

We all just gaped at Cassie. It hadn't occurred to me. It should have, but it didn't.

"Can I say something?" David asked.

"Sure," Rachel said darkly. "As long as it isn't more bad news."

"It kind of is. My dad is part of the National Security Agency. What they do is electronic surveillance. You know, like bugging phones and watching people from satellites in orbit? Well, it just seems to me the Yeerks can do all those things plus a lot more. So probably the entire Marriott resort is being watched by the Yeerks."

"I'm pretty sure I said, 'No more bad news'," Rachel grumbled. "Oh, man."

Nothing scares me more than Rachel being discouraged. By the time she starts worrying, any sane, sensible human being is ready to run screaming from the room.

"We have no choice," Jake said. "Do we?"

<If the Yeerks get to the President and these other guys, we might as well give up,> Tobias said. <Six powerful world leaders, all Controllers? I mean, those six people are just slightly more powerful than the seven of us.>

"All that security," Jake said. "That's a lot of ways to get shot."

"Yeah," Rachel agreed. "So. Let's do it."

"You ready?" Jake asked David.

David nodded.

"OK," Jake said. "This should be a nice, safe, easy trip down the coast. We're just spying the situation out. You'll need the eagle morph, but not the other morph you acquired at the zoo."

"Still, the morphing will be very creepy," Cassie warned. "So be prepared. What you do is just concentrate. Focus on the eagle."

I could see David's brow creasing with the effort of concentration.

"It's going to be weird," Rachel warned.

David's skin was already changing colour. It was turning a sort of medium brown. His eyes widened as he looked down at his hands.

"It won't hurt," I reassured him.

Lines began to appear on the brown flesh. Lines that outlined feathers. And at the same time David began to shrink.

121

"What's happening?!" he cried.

"You're getting smaller," Cassie said gently. "It's part of the process. Now the lines on your skin will deepen and go three-dimensional. You may feel itching."

"Ahhh!" he yelped as the outlines of feathers became actual feathers.

"Just hope he doesn't do that finger bone thing I did the other day," I muttered to Jake. "That'd rock his world."

Maybe I should have kept my mouth shut. Because at that exact moment, both of David's arms went shooting out, lengthening suddenly. The bones of his arm and fingers shot out, bare and white and thin as uncooked spaghetti.

"Aaaaahhh! Aaaaahhh!" David screamed.

"Eeeewww!" Rachel commented helpfully. "Now *that's* gross."

"Ride through it," Cassie said. "Just stay with it. Look! See? The flesh and feathers are covering the bones now."

Sure enough, the bones were only visible for a few seconds. But David was rattled.

"Don't sweat it," I said. "Wait till you morph a fly. You want to see disgusting? That's disgusting. This is nothing." I waved my hand dismissively.

"I don't want to—" David started to say, but then his mouth bulged out. The lips stretched, formed into a pink, fleshy beak-shape, then hardened like setting cement.

David was small now. Smaller than me. Half my size. But with enormously long, brown wings. His clothing was hanging loosely, wrinkled up around his feet. Probably a good thing. If he'd looked at his feet right then, it wouldn't have made him feel exactly better.

Then it occurred to me. "Umm, guys? David here doesn't know how to morph clothing yet. He doesn't have a morphing suit."

"Rachel and I will look away till he figures it out," Cassie said.

"We can get him something nice," Rachel said, considering. I knew in her mind she was running through the stock of every shop in the mall.

David was almost all eagle now.

"OK, now you can't talk any more," Cassie explained to him. "But you can thought-speak. Just think of who you want to talk to, whether it's me, or Marco, or all of us at once. Form the words in your mind, and we'll hear them."

<Can you hear this?>

"Yes." Cassie nodded. "See? It's easy. But now comes the really tricky part, because the eagle's brain, its basic instincts will kick in and—"

The eagle head, faintly gold in the dull grey light snapped left. The eyes focused sharply on Tobias.

The golden eagle was flapping wildly, aiming

123

sharp talons and ripping beak towards Tobias before anyone could move.

Chapter 22

David was quick. But Cassie was quick and prepared. She stepped in, expertly grabbed the flailing eagle, and held him down.

<See! See what I mean?> Tobias demanded as he retreated back up into the rafters of the barn. <Golden eagles. They're all psycho. Them and crows. And jays. And a few other birds I could mention. I mean, there are plenty of mice and rabbits to go around, no one needs to be attacking fellow birds.>

"David, David!" Cassie said. "Think, now. Focus. Your name is David. You're human. Get a grip."

The eagle flapped its wings and struggled, but even a very large bird can't fly with a girl practically riding its back. And it was still

125

entangled in David's own clothing. Slowly David calmed down.

<That was weird,> he said at last. <It was like I was myself, only suddenly there was someone else in my head, too.>

<You will become accustomed to it,> Ax said. <When I morph a human I often experience the human mind and human instincts. The need for food, for example.>

"Yeah, don't get between Ax and a cinnamon bun," I said.

"You want to try to fly?" Jake asked David.

<Fly?>

"Duh. What do you think those wings are for?" I said.

<How do I do it?>

"Well, first, wait for us all to morph. Then trust the eagle. He knows how to fly," Cassie said.

In a few minutes we were ready to take off. We left David's clothes behind in the barn.

It was strange and kind of emotional, watching someone morph for the first time. I don't know how to explain it. It was like, I don't know, like when someone becomes a citizen. You know, when they swear someone in, and one minute he's Chinese or African or Dutch or Mexican or whatever, and the next minute, once he's "solemnly sworn" or whatever, he's an American. As much an American as any other American.

I've always been kind of affected by watching that happen. I mean, my own mother was born in another country.

Anyway, that's how I felt now, watching David test out his wings. He was the new Animorph. It was official. He was one of us.

And we knew nothing about him, except that he had a snake named Spawn and a cat named Megadeth.

He flew. It wasn't a great day for flying, but we had no choice. We had to scope out the Marriott resort before all the big heavies arrived. As we flew I tried to put myself in the head of whoever was planning security for the summit. There would be roadblocks on all the roads that approached the place. There'd be snipers on the roof. Quick-response teams with heavy weapons near by. Guys with shoulder-launched anti-aircraft missiles. Stingers, I think they're called.

Amazing what you can learn by watching movies of Tom Clancy books.

They'd have boats patrolling the shoreline. Probably very fast speedboats backed up by Coast Guard cutters.

They'd probably—

<This is so excellent!> David yelled for about the tenth time, interrupting my thoughts once again. <I can see everything! I can see little crabs all the way down there on the beach! I mean, whoa!>

They'd probably have sealed up every manhole cover. They might have installed automatic locks on a lot of the doors. And of—

<Look! Look! Look at this!> David yelled as he caught a warm updraught, spread his wings, and went shooting straight up.>

<Yeah, yeah, it's cool,> I said. <But I'm trying to think here.>

David ignored me and shot past me, huge, twice my size, like a Boeing 747 jumbo jet alongside my 727. A rare glint of sun poking through the clouds flashed the muted gold of his head and neck feathers.

<Yah-haaaah!> David yelled in sheer glee.

OK, he was being annoying. But I couldn't really get mad. Flying is the coolest thing in the world. It just is. Having your own wings and being able to roam across the sky is amazing.

But I was supposed to be thinking. We had to know what to look for when we reached the resort. Had to figure out how we could move within the compound, how we were going to reach the various world leaders and spy on them. And protect them.

There were other birds in the sky, of course. And we were flying fairly far apart so, as Tobias put it, <We didn't look like some kind of bird-watcher's fantasy.>

We were spread across two kilometres or so of sky, sometimes closer together, sometimes further apart, depending on the breezes and the little pockets of dead air that'd drop you seven metres. There were geese flying fast above us, a neat V in the sky. And there were crows, gulls, and the occasional innocent hawk, all floating around below us, looking for food or just hanging out.

I didn't think anything of them, although the other birds sure noticed us. They knew the bird-of-prey silhouette. They knew they didn't want to be too close.

<Yeeee-haaaaahh!> David yelled. <I'm doing it!>

It took me a few seconds to notice that his tone sounded different. More excited. More keyed up. By the time I looked, it was too late.

David was tearing down, down, down like a falling rocket. Swooping, straight towards a careless crow.

I watched, helpless. I was an osprey. There was no way I could catch him. Golden eagles are blazingly fast. Only Jake in his peregrine falcon morph might have intercepted the eagle, but he was too far away.

With my laser-focus osprey eyes I saw the big eagle talons rake forward.

There was no sound as David struck the crow. They were too far below me for sound. Just one minute the crow was flying along, and the next second it was tumbling.

David caught the breeze again, levelled off, and swooped back upwards. The lifeless crow twirled down through the air, an unbalanced, black pinwheel.

<What are you doing?!> Jake roared.

<Um . . . um . . . I guess this eagle's brain kind of took over for a minute,> David said. <I can't believe I just did that! That poor bird! I just lost control.>

It was possible. It was hard, sometimes, to control the animal you'd morphed. So it was possible that's what had happened. The others certainly bought it. Cassie comforted him.

But I have an instinct for lies. Maybe it's because I can lie pretty well when I need to.

I know a lie when I hear one. David had killed that crow. Deliberately. In cold blood. For absolutely no reason.

<Hey, look!> Tobias said. <There's a helicopter coming up behind us. Marine Corps helicopter. It's . . . whoa! That must be Marine One!>

<Marine what?> Rachel asked.

<You know, Air Force One, the President's jet? Marine One is the President's helicopter,> Tobias explained.

<The stuff you know, Tobias,> Rachel marvelled.

I focused my osprey eyes on the helicopter. No time to worry about David. The helicopter was coming from the direction of the airport, straight towards the compound. A second, identical helicopter was about two kilometres back from the first. A decoy. Unless the first chopper was the decoy.

Then I noticed something else. A blurring in the air above and behind the helicopter. Like the air itself was swirling a little. Almost like heat waves coming up off hot asphalt.

Tobias had noticed it, too. <Oh, man! We've seen that before!>

<What's the matter?> David demanded.

<Yeerk stealth technology,> Ax said calmly. <Human eyes would never notice. Human radar won't spot it. But these eyes are very good. And Yeerk technology is, well, it's not exactly Andalite technology.>

<So what is it?> David cried.

<Yeerk spacecraft. Shielded,> I said. <One coming right up behind the President's helicopter. They aren't going to wait for the conference. The Yeerks are going after him right now!>

Chapter 23

<Move! Move! Move!> Jake yelled.

We hauled. We flapped our wings like insane ducks, racing to reach the helicopter before the Yeerks did. It was off to our side. Going the same direction as us, but still distant.

At the speed the helicopters were moving, they'd probably have reached the Marriott resort in twenty minutes. It was an hour away for us.

I could see from the dimensions of the shimmering effect that this was no little Bug fighter moving in. This was far bigger. And there was only one Yeerk ship likely to be big enough.

The Blade ship. Visser Three's personal death-dealing machine.

The shimmering air moved closer, up behind

and above the helicopter. We got closer, but we were spread out, ragged. Rachel behind with Tobias, Jake and David up front, me, Cassie and Ax more or less in the middle.

A long, narrow rectangle began to appear. It appeared in the sky as if it were just floating there. A very narrow, very long rectangle that slowly opened wider.

<The Blade ship is opening its belly hatch,> Ax said.

So. He, too, had decided this must be the Blade ship.

The hatch widened, opened, revealing the inside of the Blade ship. It was utterly bizarre. The stealth shield didn't work over the hatch itself. I could see inside. I could see a sort of inverted cradle, ready to receive the helicopter. I could see foul Taxxon heads rising from behind consoles and control panels. And I could see Hork-Bajir warriors, wearing the red uniforms they wore aboard the Blade ship.

But none of this could be seen by the helicopter. The hatch was in a blind spot above and behind. And the chase helicopter wouldn't see it, either. The angle was all wrong.

I raced. The hatch opened. I was wearing out, beating my wings against the breeze. But I was getting closer.

Suddenly, the helicopter's rotors slowed. The engine roar died out.

<They have it!> Ax yelled. <Force field is on. It killed the engines. They will probably have stunned the humans on board.>

The helicopter was almost directly above us now. From below, it looked sort of like a dark green boat as seen from underwater. There were two pylons sticking out on either side for the landing wheels.

<Aim for those pylons!> Jake said.

Jake and David soared, up and up. The rest of us went after them.

<The other chopper's going to see that this one has disappeared,> Tobias pointed out. <Even humans aren't that blind!>

But at that moment, as if in response to Tobias's warning, something new appeared. It looked as if it were a halo of light glowing all around the helicopter. But then it separated slowly, becoming distinct.

A second helicopter! It looked as if the real helicopter had shed an outer skin.

<A hologram,> Ax said grimly.

The true helicopter's rotors had come to a stop. The hatch was fully open. Up it rose. Up inside the Blade ship. And the hologram of the helicopter took its place, flying along, looking exactly like the real thing.

Jake and David soared. Jake flipped in mid-air, extended his talons, and caught an edge of one of the pylons. David grabbed a strut and

134

held on.

The hatch began to close!

<No way!> I said. I flapped till I thought my lungs would burst. Hatch closing . . . me racing . . . hatch closing . . .

I saw Cassie zip through, followed by Ax.

No time left! The hatch was closing too quickly. The opening was a metre wide . . . fifty centimetres . . . thirty centimetres . . . fifteen. . .

Zoom!

I blew through, scraping my belly and my back. A split second later, I'd have splatted. But I was in! I killed speed, twisted hard, swooped under the belly of the helicopter, and landed on the now-closed deck.

<Yes!>

I'd made it! I'd made it aboard the Blade ship of Visser Three.

Oh, goody.

What, was I insane?

Chapter 24

I was beneath the helicopter. So were Jake, Ax, Cassie and David. Rachel and Tobias were stuck outside.

Poor Rachel and Tobias.

The helicopter sat low to the ground, and since it rested in a sort of shallow depression in the deck, we were almost entirely hidden from sight.

I looked at Jake.

<Demorph,> he said tersely. <This is going to get nasty. Be ready for a fight.>

We demorphed. Within minutes we were four very scared kids and one shaky Andalite lying beneath the President's helicopter. I looked at David to see how he was maintaining. He looked like he was getting ready to visit a dentist who didn't believe in painkillers. He was ready to wet himself.

Good, I thought. *Only an idiot wouldn't be scared.*

Looking past him and the others, I could see Hork-Bajir feet rushing around the helicopter. They carried an unconscious man from the helicopter. I saw dark grey suit trousers, and black shoes. I saw the sole of one shoe. There was a slash across one heel. Like he'd stepped on something sharp.

The President? If so, we had less than zero time.

"Ax," Jake whispered. "We need a distraction."

Jake obviously thought the same. We needed time to morph.

I think if I were Ax, I might have felt just slightly resentful right then. It was like, "Ax-man, go and get yourself killed so we can take our time morphing."

But Ax is a soldier down deep inside. Smug and superior sometimes, loopy and silly other times, Ax is still an Andalite *aristh*, a warrior-in-training. And he's Elfangor's brother, which tells you a lot.

<Yes, Prince Jake, I think that would be a good idea.>

Unfortunately, it wasn't such a good idea. There was no room. Ax was squeezed in beneath

137

the helicopter's bottom. And it was suddenly obvious that none of us could go to our combat morphs in such a small space.

This was not going to come down to a quick battle. We were already too late to save the man in the slashed shoe.

"David," I whispered. His face was just centimetres from me now as he squirmed to get out of Ax's way. "Did Cassie set you up with a bug morph?"

He looked confused. "She made me touch . . . I mean, acquire . . . a cockroach. Is that what you mean?"

"Jake!" I said. "He has a cockroach morph. What do you think?"

Jake nodded. He wasn't happy, obviously. But it was the only way. We'd have to morph something small enough to get out from under the helicopter. Then worry about breaking up what ever was going on.

"OK, dude," I said to David. "We're morphing roaches. Just focus down hard, shut your eyes, and don't think about it."

So far, nothing was going well. For one thing, we didn't have Rachel or Tobias with us. For another thing, we were trapped beneath a helicopter. And for a final thing, whoever the guy with the slashed shoe was, we were going to be too late to help him.

Unless they moved awfully slowly, the Yeerks

would have plenty of time to infest him.

I assumed the slash-shoe man was the President of the United States. And man, you just don't want to think about your president being a slave of alien invaders.

If that happened, the only possible thing we could do would be to kidnap the man and keep him locked up for three days until the Yeerk in his head died from the lack of Kandrona rays.

Kidnap the President. Off an alien space-ship. And keep him hidden for three days. No problem. It's not like anyone would be looking for him. Only the ENTIRE WORLD.

Take it easy, Marco, I told myself. *One step at a time.*

I focused on the cockroach whose DNA was inside me. And I began to change.

I watched David. He was watching me, eyes showing white all around as he stared.

"Close your eyes," I said.

He did. But a second later they were open again. He was morphing, but slowly. He was shrinking quickly enough and was already no more than a metre long. And the hard brown wings were forming on his back. But the really hideous stuff hadn't started yet.

I felt my own body shrink and saw the floor expand out in every direction at once. I saw my skin grow hard and yellow-brown, like old-man fingernails. I glanced again at David. So far, so good. He was still shrinking. The roach body was taking shape. The neck was already pinched down, the wings were distinct, his arms had begun to segment, his legs likewise. He was halfway to roach.

But his face was still mostly human. Distorted, twisted, contorting as it was reconfigured to be a roach face, but his eyes were still staring white.

He'll be OK, I told myself, *as long as he gets past the extra legs.*

And just then, the extra legs appeared. First on me.

Sploot! Sploot!

They came shooting out of what had been my sides. Two big, long, hairy cockroach legs. And I guess my face probably turned roachy at that point, too, because when I next saw David it was through compound eyes.

So I saw hundreds of tiny, distorted images of him opening his mouth to scream.

And when I heard the weird, railing, moaning, horrible sound, it vibrated down my antennae.

Chapter 25

He opened his mostly human mouth to scream. It wasn't much of a scream because his lungs were almost gone. But it was enough.

A loud Hork-Bajir voice yelled, "*Hitnef shellah! Shellah!* No sound!"

Everything got very quiet. And then it was easy to hear when David screamed a second time.

"Ahhhh! Ahhhh! Ahhh!"

<Shut up, you moron!> I yelled.

<David, calm down, it's OK,> Cassie said, being somewhat more gentle than me.

"*Haff* Visser!" the Hork-Bajir voice said.

I didn't need a Hork-Bajir-to-English dictionary to figure that out. It meant "Get the Visser".

<We need to get outta here!> Jake said. <David. DAVID! Listen to me. Get a grip. Do it now. You can be hysterical some other time.>

That seemed to penetrate David's conscious-ness. He stopped screaming. But he began demorphing. He was getting more human.

<David,> Cassie said. <Listen to me. You are going to die if you don't get a grip. Finish morphing the cockroach. It's the only way.>

<No way!>

<Do it, David,> she said. <I know it's creepy, but it's better than being dead. Besides, we've all done it. Marco has done it. He's not scream-ing like a baby, is he? Aren't you as tough as Marco?>

I'd never seen this exact side of Cassie. She's always good at understanding people. It hadn't occurred to me she'd be good at manipulating people if she had to.

<You know what Marco did the first time he morphed a roach?> Cassie continued. <Just what you're doing. He freaked. But he main-tained. It's OK that you freaked. But you have to maintain now.>

I watched, and slowly, slowly David melted towards full cockroach.

Of course, now he'd really hate me. Cassie had used the tension between me and David to manipulate him. It was the right thing to do. Necessary, if we were going to live. But it was ruthless in a way, too.

Not that I had time to worry about that.

Because now the helicopter was coming up off the floor. The Yeerks were using a magnetic field to lift it and see what was underneath.

<If he can do it, I can do it,> David said at last.

I should have kept my mouth shut. But I guess I wouldn't be me if I always did the sensible thing. So I said, <When you've kicked half the Yeerk butt I've kicked, then you can talk, New-boy.>

See? Stupid. Now I'd just confirmed that David would hate me.

<Motor on outta here!> Jake yelled as the "sky" above us grew lighter. It was the helicopter rising, rising slowly up.

We hauled like only a cockroach can haul: six legs scampering madly, like Wile E. Coyote loading up to chase Roadrunner.

Zoom! Off across the steel deck.

Zoom! Over a seam in the floor that was maybe three millimetres but seemed like a wide ditch.

Zoom! My little compound eyes millimetres above the ground, my antennae waving, streaming out behind me.

Zoom! We were Vipers on the interstate! We were Porsches on the autobahn! We were like those crazy rocket cars out on the salt flats.

We were moving at full, screaming, cockroach speed.

Which, unfortunately, is about walking speed for an average adult human.

<Step on them!> Visser Three cried triumphantly. <Crush them!>

But we had one other skill, in addition to looking disgusting: we were agile little bugs. Ever try and step on a roach going full out? Ever try and step on a roach armed with full human intelligence?

It isn't easy.

WHOOOOOOOSH! Down came something so big it blocked out the sky.

I stalled the legs on my left, motored the legs on my right, and did a Bat-turn that would have left the Batmobile skidding.

BOOOOOMMMMM! A Hork-Bajir clawed foot the size of Arkansas landed behind me. Hah! Too slow.

Too slow by about three millimetres. Next one might get me.

Then. . .

<Opening up ahead here!> Jake yelled.

Opening to where? I didn't care. I saw a dark, horizontal band stretching for ever to my left and almost for ever to my right. It was just a seam between one level of steel and another, but it was taller than a coin was thick, and that's all I needed.

WHOOOOOSH!

BOOOOOMMM!

<Ahhh!> Suddenly I was running on five legs. One had been yanked out by the roots as the Hork-Bajir toe landed on it. The roach didn't care. It creeped me out, but the roach was indifferent.

We were in a two-dimensional universe. Below us, steel. Above us, pressing down on our backs, steel. We could go forward/back, and left/right. That was it. We were an Etch-A-Sketch drawing.

<Light ahead,> Ax reported.

We went for the light. But overhead was a pounding thunderstorm like nothing you've ever imagined. Dozens of humongous Hork-Bajir running above us, their massive impacts translating down through the steel. We might as well have been running around inside a drum.

BOOOM!BOOOM!BOOOM!BOOOM!

<See, isn't this fun, David?> I said, trying out a little humour. <Ah, yes, life as an Animorph. It's not a job. It's an adventure!>

All the while, the dim light ahead grew brighter. And suddenly, the pounding footsteps above us died off. We had passed beneath some kind of wall. Bulkhead, I guess it's called on a ship. Anyway, the thunder was behind us, the light ahead of us, and I was starting to experience a tiny ray of hope amidst the gibbering terror.

Say one thing for roaches: they don't wear out.

HSSSSSSSSSS.

<What's that sound?> David asked.

My whole body could feel that the hissing was behind us. And my antennae were already getting a sick, quivering feeling that they smelled something unpleasant.

I stopped. Spun towards my two-legged side and looked back. Through compound eyes I basically saw nothing. Nothing but a narrowness, a horizontal narrowness. And yet . . . something was coming nearer. I could feel it.

Something that smelled.

Something that . . .

<RAID!> I screamed. <They're gassing us!>

Chapter 26

<The light!> Ax yelled. <Go to the light!>

<If that gas reaches us we'll not only go to the light, we'll be saying "hello" to all our dead relatives and explaining our impure thoughts to Saint Peter!> I cried.

<What?> Ax asked, puzzled.

<Just RUUUUUN!>

The gas. The light. The gas. The light.

A pole, heading upwards into the light.

Zoooom! A roach shot up the pole.

Zoooom! Zoooom! Zooom!

And then me. The little roach brain, which wasn't bright enough to add two plus two, was a world-class expert at running away. I jumped, went vertical, hit that pole, and up I went. Zoooom!

The gas wave rolled by beneath me. I hauled straight up. Out into the light.

<Yeeeee-haaahhh!> I screamed in total, idiot glee at having survived. <Rachel is going to be so mad she missed this.>

We were in a very bright room. Steel floor all around, but just one distant pair of Hork-Bajir legs. And then, over my head I saw it: the Leaning Tower of Wing Tip. A gigantic shoe, cocked at an angle, totally still. It seemed so tall it was like it disappeared into the clouds. It may well have been a size thirteen.

More important, my weird-coloured, fragmented, crazy, fun-house eyeballs managed to notice that the heel had a gouge in it.

<Slash-shoe man!> I said.

<Who?> Cassie asked.

<The President of the United States!> I said. <I've always wanted to meet him. But somehow I wasn't imagining this particular scene. I thought we'd shake hands. And I figured I'd *have* hands.>

The sound of approaching steps. Strange steps.

<Something with four legs,> Ax said ominously.

That meant only one person.

<Hide!> Jake said.

<Where?> I wondered.

<Up his leg!> Cassie cried.

148

We climbed the leg of the President. Up over the polished shoe. Up across the sock. Up to the leg hair. And we cowered there beneath grey wool amidst a sparse forest of leg hairs.

Clip-clop. Clip-clop.

Hooves walked into the room.

Visser Three.

<We're out of time,> the Visser muttered to the Hork-Bajir guard. <Insects were discovered beneath the helicopter. The Andalite bandits in morph? Or just insects? Either way, no time left. I'll acquire him now.>

<Acquire?> I echoed in my mind. <Huh?>

Then it occurred to me. Slash-shoe wasn't going to be infested. Visser Three was acquiring his DNA. He wanted to be able to morph the President!

Of course! How could I have been so stupid? Like Visser Three would ever let another Yeerk take control of the most powerful human on Earth?

He was going to acquire him. Then he could become the President whenever he wanted.

Suddenly, we were moving. The Hork-Bajir was dragging Slash-shoe along the deck.

<Now what?> David asked.

<Good question,> Cassie muttered.

Slash-shoe wasn't being dragged far.

<They're putting him back on the helicopter,> Ax said. <I believe they intend to return the

helicopter to its original flight plan, replacing the hologram. They'll reverse the stun effect and all the humans on board will wake up, remembering nothing. It will be as if nothing happened.>

<I agree,> Jake said.

<Do we stay with the hairy leg here, or do we bail and maybe do some damage here on the Blade ship?> I asked.

<Bail,> Jake said. <We can't just demorph in the President's helicopter. The President won't be alone. And even if he's straight, others may not be. There could be a shoot-out.>

<So?> David said boldly. <I thought we were supposed to kick butt?>

<Not on our own President, duh,> I said.

We bailed. Down the hairy leg. Across the sock. Down the back of the shoe to drop on to the steel deck.

<Back where we started from,> Cassie remarked. <Under the helicopter.>

It took about three seconds for us all to form a mental picture of what that meant. We were standing on the hatch. The hatch that would be opened to release the helicopter.

<Uh-oh,> I said, and then, the hatch began to move beneath us. Directly beneath us. A bright line of daylight appeared in the floor not two centimetres away.

I turned to run.

The line widened.

And that's when I realized that not even a roach can outrun the wind.

The wind reached in, plucked me up, swept me into the escaping air, and sucked me down through the widening crack in the floor.

<Nooooo!> I yelled.

I saw two roaches fly past, like jets in the powerful wind.

I grabbed at the deck with my two front legs and held on. For about one millionth of a second.

And then I was falling.

Falling, twirling, twisting, down, down, down towards the ground below.

To be continued. . .

I could not stand to look at the thing.

<Marco?> I cried again. <MARCO!>

Marco trapped in some hideous, oversized flea body? And Cassie . . . what had happened to Cassie?

Suddenly, over the edge of the table, she appeared. She was fully demorphed. Her own self, even though I was still only halfway through the process.

She looked right at Marco. She placed her hands on his sides, ignoring the sting of his bristles as they poked into her skin.

The flea . . . Marco . . . tried to jump. But the legs that could fire a flea through the air were too weak to move the huge thing he had become.

"Come on, Marco," Cassie said calmly. "Clear your mind of all the fear. You can do this. You will morph. Focus on the picture of yourself. Form the picture in your mind. Let go of the fear and focus on the picture of your own body."

We were all demorphing. Rachel's head rose up above the table edge, then David, Ax. One by one they assumed their own forms. One by one they registered horror on their faces.

We all stared. Stared at the monstrous flea. And at Cassie.

And then, slowly, slowly, the armour plate began to soften into flesh. Slowly the mouthparts retreated. The spiked helmet melted into hair.

Slowly, slowly, Marco emerged.

At last he was sitting, his own self again, on the edge of the table. He looked at Cassie with his own, human eyes, and he did something I didn't think Marco was capable of. He put his arms round Cassie's shoulders and cried.

"Thank you," he whispered. "Thank you, Cassie. You saved my life."

The rest of us were left staring at Cassie with expressions you could only describe as awe.

Rachel moved close to me and whispered in my ear. "Well, that sent a few chills up my spine."

I nodded. "Oh, yeah."

"That was like some kind of miracle," David said.

Marco slid off the table and wiped away his tears with the heel of his hand. Ax sent me one of those hard-to-define Andalite smiles, something they do with their eyes alone. <I do not believe in miracles. I always said Cassie had a talent for morphing. And yet . . . this is something I have not seen before.>

"OK," Marco said, snapping us all out of our trance. "Anyone bothered to notice where we are?"

I shook myself back to reality. "Yeah. I noticed before when we flew past earlier. That's why I didn't come here. Until we had no other choice. Ax! Stay alert, keep your tail ready. Rachel? We may need some firepower."

"What the — what is all this stuff?" David wondered, looking around the room. "And look at this room! It's like, huge!"

<This, unless I am mistaken,> Ax said calmly, <is a small-scale, portable Yeerk pool.>

We were standing in one corner of the ballroom. It was three times the size of our school cafeteria. There were rows of long tables, covered in white tablecloths. Overhead were massive crystal chandeliers. A red carpet with a floral pattern was all round us. All round, except in a circle where we were standing. At each corner of the room stood a massive, ornamental marble pillar, maybe three metres in diameter.

And yet here, in one corner of the room, was

a stainless steel tub about half as big as a back garden swimming pool. Right where a pillar should have been.

"No way!" Rachel said, even as she began to morph into a grizzly bear. "Someone would have noticed, duh. There are security guys everywhere."

At that point her mouth became a muzzle.

"Rachel's right, there's no way to hide all this here," I agreed. "Unless. . ."

Ax nodded. <Yes, Prince Jake. I believe we are standing inside a hologram.>